The Coventry Carol

A DARKER MM CHRISTMAS NOVELLA

ASHLYN DREWEK

FOX HOLLOW BOOKS

For Lori — and for
all the Grinches and the
Scrooges and everyone
else who gets sad around
the holidays.
You're not alone.

Contents

Foreword

This book includes references to suicidal ideations and attempts, alcohol use, and a bit of BDSM/dubious consent. Reader discretion is advised.

Caspar

CHAPTER ONE

I fucking hated Christmas. The music, the movies, the obnoxiousness of it all. There might have been a time I liked it. But now? I had more hate for the holiday than the Grinch himself.

Funny, then, that I'd choose Christmas Eve as the perfect day to kill myself.

Not funny "ha ha," more like funny "how pathetic." But that's what I was. Pathetic. I'd had twenty-three years' worth of a useless life and it was high time it all ended.

Which is why I was standing on the railing of this frozen bridge, staring at the rush of black water beneath me and trying to work up the nerve to fucking jump.

I tipped back the bottle of whiskey and drained it, the cinnamon burning as much as the alcohol. Hopefully that would give me the courage to do what had to be done.

Forcing it down, I let the bottle dangle from my fingertips until gravity pulled it away. The empty bottle sailed through the cold air and plunged into the Dead River. I lost sight of it after that, even with the red devil on the label. The blackness swallowed it whole. I hoped it would do the same to me.

Freeze me from the inside out as I gulped frigid water into my lungs and went to sleep forever.

Tiny snowflakes swirled around me, melting against my face and bare arms. I'd walked here from my house down the road. Not even a house. More like a two-room cabin I'd scraped up enough money for as soon as I turned eighteen and got the boot from the foster care system. Happy birthday, now get the fuck out!

I hadn't bothered with a jacket mostly because I assumed I'd be dead within the hour. I hoped, anyway. I might have been in just a t-shirt and jeans, but it's not like I felt the cold. I'd been numb for so long the weather didn't affect me much. Nothing did.

It's not like there was anything keeping me here. I had no family, hence the foster care. No one I'd even call a friend. Just a town full of people who wouldn't fucking miss me. They'd miss the work I did, the carpentry skills I had, sure. But not *me*. No one gave a fuck about *me* and that was fine. That's the way it had always been and that's the way it always would be. So, better to call it quits now than piss my life away, chasing something impossible like happiness.

I grabbed onto two of the sway braces and leaned out over the water as far as I could go. All I had to do was loosen my fingers. Uncurl them from the frozen, rusty metal and fall.

"Please don't do that," a voice said next to me.

I scoffed, ignoring it. It was probably some primal part of my brain, trying to save itself from the inevitable death before it.

"No, I'm serious. I don't want you to do that."

Furrowing my brows, I slid my bleary gaze to the side and jerked back. There was a guy on the bridge next to me, his leather-gloved hands outstretched.

"Santa? Are you fucking kidding me?" I couldn't have been that drunk. Or maybe I was. I squeezed my eyes shut and opened them again, but the crimson coat trimmed in dark fur didn't disappear. Nor did the guy wearing it. Except, it wasn't an old fat guy like I was used to seeing. He couldn't have been any older than I was.

"Come down and we'll talk." He smiled, a dazzling-white smile as bright as the moonlit snow around us.

"Fuck off." I turned back to the river, letting one foot dangle over the water. Just let go, already...

"I could, but I'm not going to, Caspar."

My gaze darted back to him, narrowing to try and make out more of his face. Since Coventry, Maine had a minuscule population, I should have recognized him, but I didn't. I don't think I could have forgotten a face like that even if I tried. "Who are you? How do you know my name?"

"I know everything about you."

I scoffed again. "Doubt that."

"Your parents are dead. You spent your whole life living at the mercy of others. You have an insane talent for building things, but you never tried to pursue it beyond this small town and menial construction jobs. You want to matter to someone. I'm telling you, you do. But you have to get down off that railing."

Every word he said was like an icicle to my heart. Who the fuck did this guy think he was? I didn't come out here for a fucking life lesson. I came out here to die. And now I couldn't even do that in peace.

Instead of listening to him, I let go of one of the sway braces and grabbed the other with both hands. Swinging myself in an arc around it, I stepped onto the railing directly in front of him. "The fuck you gonna do about it, Santa? Make me?"

The concern on his face melted, replaced with a smirk. "If I have to."

"And if I told you to suck my dick?"

"I'd tell you to take it out." Undeterred, he climbed up onto the railing in front of me, his hands wrapping around mine on the metal braces. Up close he smelled like pine trees and peppermint. "If that's what it takes to get you down from here, I'll suck whatever you want me to."

Maybe dying could wait another day. I mean, who'd pass up an offer like that? It didn't matter he was a total stranger in the middle of the woods on fucking Christmas Eve. Nothing mattered, so why should that?

"Who are you?" I asked again, trying to focus on his eyes in the moonlight. It was too dark to make out a color, but they glittered in a way that was mesmerizing. Or I was just completely blitzed.

"The person asking to take you home." He removed one hand from the brace and slipped it around my waist. I swallowed thickly but didn't object, which he must have taken as permission to do the same with the other, until I was the only thing keeping both of us anchored to the bridge. "Let's go home, Caspar."

I watched his lush mouth form the words but I barely heard what he was saying. I was too busy wondering if the peppermint I smelled was actually coming from him or if it was my drunken imagination at work. The only way to find out was to taste those lips, so I did.

Slanting my mouth to his, I ran my tongue across his pouty lips, thrilled when my tongue came away with a minty sensation. After all the cinnamon, the mint was refreshing.

His gloved hands twisted in my t-shirt, pulling me against him as he opened his mouth and licked into mine. Even his tongue tasted like peppermint. I let go of the brace so I could thread my fingers through his hair and grip the back of his head, kissing him as hard as I could, like I could lick all that peppermint away if I only tried hard enough.

Moaning into the kiss, he loosened one hand from my

shirt and reached for my other hand. Without even thinking, I gave it to him. By the time I realized I wasn't holding onto the bridge, we were falling.

I braced for a shock of cold — either freezing water or the mound of snow piled up on the side of the bridge. The wind rushed by, sharp and stinging, but the crushing impact never came.

Instead, I somehow landed in my bed, next to the crackling fireplace in my house.

"What just happened?" I looked up at the guy straddling my lap, trying to figure out how the hell we went from the bridge to my bed in the time it took me to blink.

He peeled off the heavy, fur-lined coat he was wearing and tossed it onto a chair. The clothes underneath looked like he wandered away from a Renaissance faire — a black billowy shirt with gold embroidery and crimson pants. Maybe he was an actor or something. I didn't really care because from the looks of things, he wouldn't be wearing clothes much longer.

"Nothing yet," he replied, leaning down to kiss me again. His warm hands held either side of my face, since he'd somehow managed to ditch the fancy gloves too.

The way he kissed me made my toes curl. I definitely wasn't imagining the peppermint flavor. It was still on his tongue as it swirled with mine.

Tugging his shirt out of his waistband, I slid my hands up his back, remembering a second too late that my palms were rough as hell. But he somehow knew what I did for a living, so he must have expected some calluses.

Either way, he didn't seem to mind since he ground against my dick with his own hard-on, groaning into my mouth.

I moved my hands down his sides and gripped his waist, holding him in place while I thrust up against him. He broke the kiss with a gasp, swiveling his hips against me with a hungry gleam in his eyes.

"I want to fuck you," I said against his lips, thrusting again in the vain attempt to get more friction for both of us. "Whoever you are."

"Nick."

"Nick," I repeated, kissing him again and sucking his plush, lower lip into my mouth. I did want to fuck him, but I could have also been happy kissing him all night.

He pushed away from me so he could sit up and take his shirt off. I didn't know why I ever thought he was Santa. He was tall and lean, with abs Santa could only fucking dream about. I ran my hand over the muscles, tracing the rigid lines up to his smooth chest.

Helping tug my t-shirt over my head, Nick promptly stretched out along my body, kissing me again. The feel of him was otherworldly. It may have been that I was so cold from being outside earlier, but his golden skin felt like the sun against me, warm and soft and comforting. Guess I should have taken a jacket after all.

Wrapping my arms around him, I rolled us to the side and settled on top of him, pressing kisses to his throat. He tipped his head back with a sigh, running his fingers through my dark hair.

I licked and sucked my way across his chest until I got to his nipple. Flicking it with my tongue, I teased it until it hardened. I sucked and nibbled it until Nick was squirming beneath me, rolling his hips up against mine.

I did the same thing to his other nipple, except this time I slid my hand down his abs and palmed his hard-as-steel cock over his pants. There was already a wet spot on the front as he thrust against my palm, panting and whimpering.

"You're just ready to go, aren't you?" I asked, dragging my

tongue down the sculpted lines of his body until I was settled between his legs.

"You have no idea." He ran his fingers through the longer part of my hair and pulled me forward so I could mouth his hard-on through his pants. I sucked at the wet spot, adding my saliva to the dampness.

I didn't torture him for long, because torturing him was torturing me and I really wanted to taste his cock. Nosing along the side of it, I inhaled more of the piney scent on my way up to unbutton his pants. He lifted his ass so I could pull them off easily.

"No underwear? What exactly were you planning for tonight?" I smirked at the sheepish smile on his face and turned my attention to the hard-on right in front of me.

I might have been drunk, but even still, it was the most beautiful thing I think I'd ever seen. Pretty sure it was bigger than mine, but I didn't care. Being that perfect, it had every right to be the biggest cock in the room.

Dragging my tongue across the slit, I collected the pre-cum gathered there with a sigh. It might have been my imagination, but I swear every part of him tasted like a goddamn candy cane. "Fuck you taste good."

"Wasn't I supposed to be the one sucking you?" His hips jerked as I wrapped my lips around his shaft and slid down it as far as I could go.

The thought of him sucking me off with those perfect, red lips was almost enough to make me come on the spot. I groaned, sliding my mouth up and down his length, licking and massaging it with my tongue. What I couldn't reach with my mouth, I stroked with my hand, mindful not to be too rough with the calluses on my palm.

"Be rough with me," Nick sighed, like he could read my thoughts. "Use me, Caspar. Do whatever you want."

I popped off the end of his dick but kept stroking it.

When I looked up, he was biting his lower lip, his eyes half-hooded as he watched me slip out of my jeans and toss them to the side.

"You want it rough?" I asked, shifting forward to stroke our lengths together in my palm, smearing my saliva and pre-cum over both of us.

Nick nodded and licked his lips, his breath coming faster.

"Roll over. On all fours."

As soon as he did, I grabbed both ass cheeks and spread him open as wide as he could go. Spitting at his hole, I buried my face against his ass, licking the furrowed skin around his entrance with abandon. His moans and gasps drove me to kiss and suck even harder, dragging my tongue from his hole to his balls and back again.

Every now and then, I'd kiss his ass cheeks, squeezing them and giving them just as much attention. I used every part of my lips and nose and chin that I could to draw out the sounds of his pleasure. It was the giving season, after all, and just hearing him was almost enough to make me come.

He pushed back against me, threading his fingers through my hair and pulling my mouth against his hole again. I drove my tongue into him, licking as far as I could while he gave a strangled cry.

The bed was practically drenched between our leaking cocks and all of the excess saliva. I didn't care. It was about to get messier.

I rose up on my knees behind him and aligned my cock with his hole, teasing him with the head. Pushing in a bit, I backed off again to smear the silvery strands of pre-cum around his rim. Working up even more spit in my mouth, I let it drop onto his hole and watched it slip inside him. "Fuck, that's hot."

"Fuck me, Caspar. Please."

I was all too happy to accommodate that breathy request.

Pushing the head of my cock against him slowly, it had my complete attention as it disappeared inch by glorious inch. "Oh my God. Your ass is fucking perfect."

Nick moaned and flicked his hips backward, taking the rest of me in with little whimpers and moans until I bottomed out inside of him.

Grasping him by his hips, I pulled out slowly, almost all the way, before thrusting in again. He gasped, his fingers digging into the flannel sheets.

"Again."

I did as he asked, pulling out until just the tip remained before slamming back into him.

He moaned, nearly every muscle in his body tensing. "Just like that."

I did the same thing, again and again, gradually picking up the pace until I was pounding into him. The sound of our bodies smacking together, combined with our frantic grunts and groans, filled the cabin until I was sure everyone in Coventry would be able to hear us out here. Ask me if I cared.

Seizing a handful of Nick's blond hair, I pulled his head backward, forcing him to arch his back to relieve the pain. "You had enough yet?"

He shook his head, hissing when I tightened my hold. "It'll never be enough."

I pushed his head down and pulled out of him slowly. Flipping him onto his back, I captured his lips with mine, kissing him as ruthlessly as I'd fucked him. If he was a glutton for more, I'd give him more. I'd give him all that I had.

He twined his arms around my neck at the same time he wrapped his legs around my waist, pulling me against him. I was guaranteed to get him to orgasm with our new position. The slight up curve of my dick meant his prostate was mine for the taking while we were face-to-face.

Tearing myself away from his peppermint lips, I pushed

myself upright and sank inside of him again. Keeping one of his legs over my shoulder, I planted kisses up and down his calf while moving in and out of him at a much slower pace.

I know he said he wanted it rough, but I was totally stealing a moment to be selfish. Seeing him laid before me, watching the firelight dance over his skin, was like a fucking dream — a dream I didn't want to wake up from. He raked his teeth across his lower lip, gazing up at me with lust-drunk eyes. I wanted to commit everything about him to memory, from the way his lashes fluttered shut when I thrust deep inside him; to the way he tasted; to the way he moaned and sighed my name.

He reached for one of my hands. When I gave it to him, he brought it to his mouth and dragged his tongue across my palm, making it nice and wet before he wrapped my fingers around his cock.

Once again, I was happy to oblige whatever he wanted. Thrusting into him and stroking him at the same time, I felt a twisted sort of pride unfurl inside my chest when his eyelids sank closed and he clawed at the sheets.

"I'm so close," he breathed, his chest heaving as he writhed beneath me, matching my thrusts with his own.

I let a drop of spit roll past my lips and spread it over his cock with each stroke. My own relief was on the horizon. Each time he clenched around my dick, my balls drew up a little tighter, the pressure built a little more, until I was as desperate as he was.

"Kiss me," Nick panted, shifting his leg off my shoulder.

As soon as I leaned down, he seized my face with both hands and ravaged my mouth. I felt him tremble a moment before he cried out against my lips. His cum sprayed out, coating his stomach and my hand in equal parts. I continued fucking him through each wave of his orgasm, his muscles clamping around my cock, squeezing me until my own release exploded within me.

Breathing hard, I stretched out carefully along his body, making sure to balance my weight so I didn't crush him or anything. He ran his fingers through my hair lazily while I kissed his jaw, his throat, down the side of his neck, anywhere I could reach. I couldn't get enough of that fucking peppermint I tasted.

When I glanced at him, he gave me a small, sleepy smile and brushed his nose against mine, an innocent gesture, a thousand times more intimate than I would have expected after a hookup like that.

"I'm glad we met tonight," I said softly, studying the depth of his dark blue eyes, trying like hell to recall if I'd ever seen him before.

"I'm glad you listened."

"Where'd you come from, anyway?"

"The North Pole, silly. Isn't that where Santa is supposed to live?" He smiled brightly, his body rocking with quiet laughter beneath me.

"Oh, so he's cute *and* he thinks he's funny," I said with a shake of my head, failing to stop a smirk before it formed.

"I know I'm funny," he countered with a grin.

"We'll see." I rolled off of him and retrieved a wet washcloth from the bathroom. After cleaning him up, I crawled back into bed and tugged the damp top sheet off. Wadding it into a ball, I tossed it over the foot of the bed and slipped beneath the comforter, pulling it up over both of us.

Nick laid down next to me on his side, watching me with a pensive expression.

"What's wrong?" I asked, mirroring his pose. Frankly, I was surprised he was still there. Usually guys bolted as soon as they were done, but he didn't look like he was in any hurry to go. And for some reason I couldn't explain, I was more than ok with him staying.

"I'm worried about what's going to happen when I leave."

"What do you mean?"

"I don't want to see you on that bridge again."

"Oh." I swallowed thickly and dropped my gaze from his. The alcohol may have worn off, but the embarrassment was still there. How fucking pathetic *was* I? I couldn't even kill myself like I'd planned, and then I'd gone and ruined this guy's night. Because I'm sure a pity lay was exactly what he wanted to do for Christmas Eve. He probably had some festival to get to or something, which would explain the old-timey Santa outfit.

"Will you make me a promise?" he asked, his fingertips ghosting over my cheek.

I glanced up but didn't say anything. I wasn't promising anything until I heard what the terms were.

"One year. Give me one year before you try anything like that again."

He looked so serious all I could do was nod. I honestly didn't know if I'd ever try it again. Failing once already was a kick in the balls I wasn't expecting. Then again, I wasn't expecting a hot stranger to be on that bridge either.

The clock on the mantel chimed twelve times, the only sound in the cabin beside the crackling logs in the hearth beneath it.

"Merry Christmas, Caspar," Nick whispered before his lips pressed to mine.

BLINKING MYSELF AWAKE, I GLARED AT THE BLEAK December sunlight slicing through the curtains. My head was fucking killing me. Guess that was my fault for downing an entire bottle of Fireball and not drinking *any* water before bed. You think I'd know better by now.

Shivering, I pulled the blanket around myself even tighter and glanced over at the fireplace. At some point in the night it had gone out, leaving the room so cold I could see my breath. I knew I'd have to get up eventually, but for the time being, I burrowed deeper under the covers.

Fragmented memories of a guy with blue eyes flashed in my brain. Images of Santa and the old bridge over the Dead River were there too, making everything a jumbled mess of whiskey and regret. Was he real? He couldn't have been. But he *felt* real.

For some reason, my attention turned to the empty space in bed next to me. There was an impression in the center of the pillow, like someone had been sleeping there. Laying my hand over it, I furrowed my brow at the cool cotton. I probably just rolled over in my sleep. That explained it.

I propped myself up on my elbow and glanced around the room, looking for any sign someone else was with me or had been. After a moment of seeing nothing, I shook my head and laid down again.

"What a weird fucking dream."

Only later, when I forced myself to get out of bed did I see it — a snow globe, sitting next to the clock. Not a cheap one made of plastic that played annoying, commercial Christmas music. This one was... old. Ornate. It had a heavy, metal base sculpted in beautiful, swirling designs and was inlaid with crystals that looked like snowflakes. Inside was an equally stunning ice castle, surrounded by mountains and a forest of evergreens.

I carried the snow globe back to my bed and sat, holding it

in my hands. Where the fuck did it come from? Given how I felt about Christmas, I knew I sure as shit didn't buy it. I had zero decorations — for *any* holiday. About the most festive I got was switching up the type of whiskey I imbibed. Even if I was going to suddenly start decorating (which I wasn't) it wouldn't be for Christmas and I certainly wouldn't go for a fucking snow globe.

Merry Christmas, Caspar.

My dream guy's voice whispered in the back of my mind. I could almost taste peppermint on my lips.

"Sleep, you idiot. You need more sleep." I set the snow globe on my nightstand and shimmied back underneath the covers, forcing my eyes shut. Hopefully the next time I woke up, this wretched day would be over.

Nick

~~~

CHAPTER TWO

"I hope that's a woman you're looking at, Nicholas," Father said, eyeing me over the top of his half-moon glasses.

It wasn't. It most certainly wasn't, but I would never admit that. I'd been dodging the issue for five years already. Christmas only seemed to make it worse — reminding my father that I still hadn't married or even shown one inkling of interest in a future wife. It's not like he was retiring anytime soon, so I don't know why it was such a big deal, but every year we had the same argument. It was our own twisted Christmas tradition and I hated it.

Forcing myself to turn away from the snow globe overlooking Caspar's part of the world, I faced Father with a bitter smile. "If you insist I take over one day, then shouldn't I know how all of this works? I think that's more important than picking some random woman to be my wife."

He didn't look convinced, but he didn't push the issue, either, and resumed reading the paper in front of him. With a huff, he leaned forward and dipped his pen in an ink well, scratching out a name from the Nice List. I knew without looking the name transferred itself to the *other* list. Poor kid.

I tamped down my irritation and turned back to the massive wall of snow globes. Zeroing in on Caspar's again, I squinted as a tiny version of him rushed around the inside of his house. He picked up his own miniature snow globe and ran a dust rag over it. Before he set it down on his nightstand, his brows furrowed and he shook it, stirring up the glittery snowflakes.

I wished I could have stayed with him that night. As soon as he fell asleep, I crept out of his bed and dressed quickly. If Father knew where I was, on Christmas Eve of all nights, I knew I'd face his wrath. But I didn't care. Caspar had been worth it. I'd make the same choice a hundred times and never regret it.

Despite knowing his hatred for the holiday, I couldn't leave Caspar's without giving him *something*. Except, I had nothing. I'd left home in such a hurry all I had were the clothes on my back and—the snow globe!

Leaving it behind was another risk, but one I was willing to take. I'd get a replacement as soon as I got home, and this way Caspar would have something in the morning, something *real*, not more disappointment.

Setting the snow globe on the mantel, next to the clock, I gave him one final look before I slipped away into the darkness.

In the days that followed, Caspar convinced himself I was a dream and nothing more. But he kept the snow globe. Sometimes, when I checked in on him, I'd see him sitting in bed with it, just staring at it. Could he see me, the way I could see him? I doubted it. He was mortal, after all. Perhaps he was pondering how it came to be in his house? Perhaps he wondered where all the little gifts came from over the following months.

One day at work, one of his thick leather gloves fell out of his back pocket. He didn't notice until he got home. After tearing apart his truck and his toolbox, he angrily concluded it was gone.

The next morning, he woke to a new pair laying on his kitchen table.

The same thing happened when I overhead part of a conversation he was having with a coworker, discussing some new tool on the market. As soon as he was asleep, I left it for him on the table, thoroughly enjoying his confused delight when he found it.

His truck was always filled with gas, just as his refrigerator never ran out of food.

Leaving him nominal tokens of my affection was the only way I could let him know I was still there, even if I wasn't *there*. He wasn't alone, like he thought. If I couldn't be with him, I could at least make sure he was taken care of in whatever capacity he needed.

Unfortunately, I had to stop for a while. When Caspar scheduled a doctor's appointment, concerned over his sudden bought of "memory loss," I forced myself to lay low. It was hard, though. He'd been a constant part of my life for years before I ever introduced myself on that fateful night.

I was just a child when I first heard his name — Caspar Payne. Father was going through the Naughty List again right before Christmas, making last-minute changes. Caspar was on the list, as he would be for the next several years until he was blacklisted altogether as a nonbeliever.

But just because he was blacklisted, didn't mean I couldn't still make sure he was ok. In fact, it seemed to me he needed even *more* attention because, at the end of the day, he had no one. Except me.

Caspar wasn't a bad person, he simply hated Christmas. He'd never been given a reason *not* to hate it. Society teaches children to expect certain things when it comes to holidays and he'd been left disappointed year after year until he deemed it was all a lie. Christmas wasn't the most wonderful time of the year — it was the loneliest, whether you were surrounded by people or not.

Orphaned young, moved from one foster home to the next, he was swept along in life by people who didn't want him. But *I* wanted him. I wanted to give him everything he'd missed his entire life. But more than doling out trivial presents, I wanted to show him someone cared. Except I couldn't. Because I was here and he was... *there*.

When I saw him on the bridge that night, I broke every single protocol there was, Father's wrath be damned. Everything that happened later was, without a doubt, the best night of my life.

Until I left.

Forced to return to my frozen existence, wilting in my father's shadow, I resumed my duties as the eldest son with silent bitterness.

Christmas had changed and it had changed my father. It wasn't about being with the people you cared about or sharing a meal or decorating a tree. Now it was about acquiring mass quantities of meaningless gifts in order to showcase your wealth and status. The world had moved beyond the simplicity of what Christmas used to be and turned it into a veritable machine, one that never stopped running.

My father embraced the change, meanwhile, I loathed it. Christmas no longer held any magic for me — except for the brief time I shared with Caspar. Those forbidden minutes, totaling naught but a few hours of his life, meant more to me than I could have ever imagined. Suddenly, I had a purpose and my purpose was *him*.

"Are you coming with me to the workshop later?" Father asked behind me.

Blinking myself back to the present, I looked up at the snow globe in time to see Caspar open the front door and let someone in. My lip curled when I saw it was another guy — Ryan. He was tall and blond and had been coming around with increasing frequency. Every time I saw him an unspeakable rage erupted inside of me.

I almost didn't answer Father, but I forced myself to clear my throat. "Of course." What else was I going to do? Spy on Caspar and his... guest?

"Good."

Ryan didn't waste any time throwing himself into Caspar's arms, kissing him as if his life depended on it.

Caspar responded with enthusiasm, which tripled the hurt inside of me.

It was irrational, I know. I'd told myself a hundred times to leave Caspar alone, to stop watching over him. Even now, I screamed at myself to walk away, but I couldn't. I stayed glued to the spot, watching Ryan rip Caspar's jeans open and free his rapidly hardening cock. He devoured it in no time, using his hand and mouth to pleasure the man of my dreams. I could just hear Caspar now — the moaning and the gasps.

In spite of myself, my cock twitched. I licked my lips and stole a cautious glance over my shoulder. As usual, Father wasn't paying me the least bit of attention. Before I lost my nerve, I swiped the snow globe and hid it at my side. "I've seen enough for today," I said, putting on the best bored tone I could manage. "I'll meet you later."

"If you see your brother, you might as well send him up. It would be good for him to get out of that forge and learn more important things. You know. Just in case."

Clenching my teeth, I ignored his not-so-subtle dig and hurried out of his office.

By the time I made it to my bedroom with the snow globe, Caspar and Ryan had stripped one another naked.

"Don't," I whispered, but to whom, I wasn't sure. It could have been meant for any one of the three of us — or all of us.

Still, angry as I was, I couldn't help but palm my rigid cock at the sight of Caspar naked. Dark hair, dark eyes, every part of him sharp and defined from years of manual labor. His hands were so rough, but the rest of him was soft and silky to the touch.

I closed my eyes for a moment, pretending my hand was his. Spitting into my palm, I shoved it down my pants and fisted my cock. I stroked myself as Ryan climbed on top of Caspar and sank down onto the dick of the man I was so desperate for. I hated every second of what I was seeing, but I couldn't look away.

Caspar closed his eyes and thrust upwards, his fingers digging into Ryan's hips. Was it Ryan he was picturing? Or someone else?

As soon as the tiny hope came to light, I snuffed it out. Of course it was Ryan he was imagining. It was Ryan's body he was feeling, Ryan's skin he was tasting. No one else's. The thought that it might be was ludicrous.

I watched as Caspar held him steady and fucked into him from below, hard and fast, the way I'd wanted it. I had no idea why. Maybe because I heard Caspar thinking about things being rough and I thought that's what *he* wanted. Either way, it had been amazing — something I'd truly been dreaming about since Caspar was sixteen and I caught my first glimpse of him masturbating in the shower. At that moment, a switch in my brain was flipped and there was no turning back. I couldn't look at girls the same way. I couldn't even look at any other guy. Caspar was the only one I saw and the only one I wanted.

Muffled moaning came through the snow globe beside me. Ryan threw his head back, balancing on Caspar's taut abs. His face twisted with ecstasy while mine darkened in anger.

It had been months, but I still remembered how it felt to have Caspar inside me. To be stretched and filled and *used* by him. I wanted that feeling again but more than that, I didn't want Ryan having it — or anyone else. Nor did I want anyone else even attempting to replace Caspar. Like a wife. He was the only one I'd ever been with in that regard and he was the only one I *wanted* to be with.

Caspar flipped Ryan around and climbed up behind him. My mouth practically watered at what was coming next. Twisting and stroking my cock, I watched as Caspar pumped in and out of Ryan's ass. His eyes were closed again and he bit his lip. I could tell he was close, as close as I was.

"Oh, yeah... do it, Caspar." I barely had any lubrication on my hand anymore, except the pre-cum which kept getting wiped away with every furious stroke. I didn't mind the added friction. In a way, it reminded me of Caspar's palm.

As soon as his hips stuttered and he gave a strangled cry, I knew he'd finally come. The memory of his cock pulsating inside me tipped me over the precipice. I had just enough time to shove my pants out of the way, catching most of my release in my hand, save for the drops that fell back onto my lower abdomen.

"Fuck." Breathing hard, I laid there for a minute, caught up in the blissful haze of that night as well as my present-day orgasm. As soon as my skin started getting itchy, I pulled my shirt over my head and cleaned myself off. Proper bathing could wait a minute.

Rolling onto my side, I dragged the snow globe closer, cradling it as it lay next to me.

I didn't know if I should be happy or angry that Ryan was already headed toward the door, giving Caspar a brief kiss at the threshold. It seemed rude, but I also didn't want to see Caspar wrapping his arms around someone else in the intimate moments that were supposed to come after sex. He and Ryan never seemed to cuddle, but I wasn't sure why.

Caspar pushed the door shut after him and walked back to his bed, collapsing on top of it. He laid there for a while, staring at the ceiling with an unreadable expression before he rolled over and grabbed something off the nightstand.

Settling back into bed, he shook his hands and stared at whatever he was holding.

I squinted, trying to see what it was.

After a minute, he shifted onto his side and set his snow globe on the bed next to him, resting it carefully against the pillow where I'd once lain.

A smile stretched across my face and a flutter raced through my stomach. I knew right then I was going to see him again, no matter how many of Father's rules I had to break along the way.

Caspar

CHAPTER THREE

Dumping an armful of firewood onto the pile next to the cabin, I stacked the pieces before trudging back to the stump to continue splitting the rest of it. The late-afternoon sun beat down through the mostly-bare trees, so hot it felt like a spotlight was on me. Spring was late this year. It seemed Winter didn't want to let go until we were nearly into May.

Sweat continued to roll down my back, despite the fact I'd ditched my coat and t-shirt with the last load. I wiped the perspiration off my forehead with the back of my gloved hand and set up the next log on the stump. In one smooth swing, I brought the axe down, watching the split pieces fall into their separate piles. It was an oddly satisfying feeling. All manual labor for me was. It was a testament to my own strength, my own abilities, the fact I didn't have to rely on anyone for anything.

You have an insane talent for building things.

I shook my head and rolled my shoulders back before propping up the next piece of wood. That fucking voice again. It came at me when I least expected it. For the life of me, I couldn't figure out who the hell it was. I never knew my dad, so it clearly wasn't him. None of the assholes in the foster care system would bother noticing anything about kids in their house unless it was directly tied to the checks the State gave them.

As far as I was aware, no one really knew about any of the shit I made. Every once in a while someone in Coventry would commission me to build something random — tables, chairs, dressers, even a bed one time. But it's not like I advertised my work. It wasn't a job — it was just something I did whenever there was a lull in the housing market and I needed the cash.

You have to get down off that railing.

Slamming the axe through the next piece of wood, I left it lodged in the stump and stepped over the pile, abandoning the task. For some inexplicable reason, I had to go to the bridge right.the.fuck.now. Maybe it would finally shut that voice up.

I hadn't been to the bridge since Christmas Eve, even if it meant taking a longer route to avoid it. Mostly it was embarrassment that kept me away, not wanting to be reminded of the fact I'd had a plan — a shitty plan, but a plan nonetheless — and I'd failed to see it through. But also there was that fucking voice again, going off in the back of my head like an alarm anytime I thought about the bridge.

Please don't do that.

Waking up on Christmas morning, I had a vague recollection of being on the bridge the night before, so I knew I at least made it that far. But everything after was... jumbled. There were moments that felt *so* real and others that were clearly an indication of how much alcohol I had put away.

Yanking my t-shirt on, I wandered down the gravel driveway and followed the road to my destination. Maybe by growing some balls and finally going back to the bridge, I'd be able to figure out what the fuck my problem had been over the past few months.

The doctors said I was fine. There wasn't a tumor growing in my brain or anything. They checked. But my mom had been a junkie before she OD'ed. Maybe she passed that shit onto me when I was born and now I was on an extended acid trip or something. Or maybe the crack was finally short-circuiting my brain. I don't know.

There had to be a reason I was losing my fucking mind. Shit kept appearing in the house without me buying it — or remembering that I bought it, at any rate. I couldn't even tell you the last time I put gas in my truck. I took it to the mechanic to make sure the fuel gauge was still working. It was. I was just fucking nuts, apparently.

My boots thumped across the old bridge platform, accompanied by the rush of water down below and the wind as it whistled through the tops of the trees. I forgot how pretty it was out here, even without the snow. The fact it was in the middle of nowhere, without a soul in sight, made it even better.

Bracing my forearms against the railing, I stared out over the river, watching the water flow into the distance and disappear around the bend. That was supposed to be me. I was supposed to disappear, too.

You want to matter to someone.

I scoffed at the words. Wrong again, little voice. I didn't "want" to matter to anyone because I knew it was never going to happen. So why want something you can't have? That was a recipe for disappointment and I'd had enough of that to last a lifetime.

Even Ryan was a disaster waiting to happen. He hadn't figured it out yet, but there was no life with me. Not now, not ever. There wouldn't be a happily ever after for us because they didn't fucking exist. So we met, we fucked, and we went our separate ways until the next time one of us was horny.

That was the best it was ever going to be. I didn't have the ability to give him anything more.

"You should just do it," I muttered out loud. I don't know why I made myself some stupid promise to wait until next Christmas. Who was holding me accountable? Me? Well *Me* wanted to die, so who gave a fuck if it was now or eight months from now? Why did I keep hanging on? Maybe it was because I was scared to die, even though it hurt so much to keep living.

Hauling myself up onto the railing, I grabbed onto the sway braces on either side of me. The sun was already starting to set, but I could still make out the huge rocks in the river below. All the melting snow meant the water was higher than usual, but from this vantage point I could see everything clearly. If I was lucky, I'd end up cracking my head open against one of them and *then* I'd drown, since this time around I wouldn't be essentially paralyzed by freezing water on impact.

I teetered on the edge of the rusting metal, swaying with the wind as it pushed me to and fro. I couldn't even blame the alcohol for hesitating this time. This was pure cowardice.

"You're not a coward," the little voice said.

"Oh, shut the fuck up." I closed my eyes, trying to ignore it. "I should have done this in December. Instead, I dragged it out. And for what? Hoping life would get better?" I snorted and shook my head.

"It will get better. I'll do whatever it takes to make it better."

"It's a little late now. The bar keeps moving. First, it was, 'Oh, it'll get better once you're adopted.' Except no one wants a fucking six-year-old. They want babies. Then it was, 'Oh, it'll get better in a *nice* foster home.' Then, 'Just make it to graduation' and 'Just make it to twenty-one.' Now? Now, what the fuck do I have? At what milestone is life going to magically get better? Huh?! Because from where I'm standing, it doesn't! And I'm fucking tired. I'm so tired."

I leaned my forehead against my arm and squeezed my eyes even tighter, but the tears slipped out anyway. The gusting wind practically dried them on the spot. Unfortunately, it wasn't strong enough to push me off that railing and I wasn't strong enough to let go.

"I know," the voice said sadly. "I know you're tired and you're hurting. But you promised me. Please don't break that promise. Please, Caspar. Get down."

"I came here to see if I could remember what happened that night," I said, blinking away my tears and focusing on the river again. "To see if I could figure out why I didn't jump the first time. And why my guardian angel was in a fucking Santa coat."

"And?"

"I don't have a fucking clue, except I must be batshit since I'm standing out here talking to myself. *Again*."

"Only, you're not talking to yourself. If you'd bothered to look, you'd see I'm right here."

A second later, a man's hand reached up and covered mine on the brace. He planted his boots on either side of my feet and snaked one arm around my torso, pulling me back against him so I couldn't fall no matter how much I thought I wanted to.

"Who the fuck are you?" I asked, still not turning around. Another breeze swept past us, stirring up the familiar scent of peppermint and pine needles. I was really fucking losing it now. It was the same hallucination from that night. It had to be some latent acid in my fat cells or brain cancer or some shit. There's no other way to explain how something could feel so real, *twice*, when it wasn't.

"I told you. I'm the person asking to take you home. The one who's begging you to get down."

"You're not real." I shook my head, closing my eyes again.

"I am. Look at me."

Relenting, I turned as best I could, studying him over my shoulder. A flood of memories hit me hard, like a sucker punch to the gut. The way his gold hair felt in my hand; the way he tasted; the way it felt just to hold him and breathe in the wintry smells on his skin. "Nick?"

He flashed a stunning smile before his lips were on mine.

I melted against him, losing myself in his kiss. The arm around me loosened and plucked my hand free from the brace. Lacing his fingers through mine, he wrapped both of our arms around my waist. I didn't even pay attention to the fact his other hand was already prying my fingers off the brace until the sensation of falling shot through my stomach.

Except, this time we didn't mysteriously crash land in my bed — or the river. We both landed on our feet on the bridge. Nick spun me to face him completely and kissed me in earnest, his hands diving into my hair and angling my head for a deeper kiss.

For a moment, I relished the feeling of his mouth on mine, savoring all the warm memories from our first meeting. Then the cold reality set in and I shoved him away from me.

"Who the fuck do you think you are?" I balled my hands at my sides, resisting the urge to fucking punch him and the offended look right off his face.

"What? What do you mean?"

"I've spent the last four months thinking you were some fucked-up wet dream and now, all of a sudden, you're here again? What the fuck? Where have you been? If you were going to fuck and run, fine. But stop coming around and sticking your nose in where it doesn't belong!"

"Caspar." He reached for my face but I jerked away from him, my lip curling.

"Don't act like you fucking care."

Somehow he looked even more wounded than before, his blue eyes soft and glassy. "I *do* care."

"How is it you're always here? Huh? Do you just hang out at bridges all day for fun?"

"I'm here for you."

"Are you fucking stalking me?" Taking a step forward, my eyes narrowed on his. I couldn't help but notice he was wearing the same medieval-y looking clothes as last time, except this shirt was pure white with silver embroidery, paired with navy blue pants. Come to think of it, he looked like a prince out of a fairytale — if princes spent their days stalking nobodies in the middle of nowhere.

Nick swallowed, but held his ground, his chin tipped up in his defense. "It's not like that."

"Then what the fuck is it like?" He still didn't budge, even after I came nose-to-nose with him, searching his face for some sort of explanation.

"Can we go back to your place and talk?"

"We can talk right here. You can start by answering my questions."

"What do you want to know?"

"What the fuck are you doing here?"

"I told you, I'm here because of you. I saw you here again and I got scared. You made a promise, Caspar."

"And how the hell do you know my name?"

He swallowed again, his gaze darting about like he was looking for the right answer. "That part is more complicated. I want to tell you. I want to tell you everything, but I can't."

"Stay the fuck away from me." The words were out of my mouth before my heart or my brain could reel them back in. His face registered shock and pain all at once. Strangely, the same visceral reaction clawed through the center of my chest. But it was too late now.

Pivoting on the heel of my boot, I strode away from him as

fast as I could. So much for figuring out what my problem was. Guess it wasn't a total loss, though. Coming out here had confirmed Nick *was* real and apparently he was fucking crazy. But it also confirmed I was a giant pussy who talked the talk but couldn't walk the walk. Maybe instead of flinging myself off a bridge, I'd work up the nerve to go lay down in front of a train. That ought to do the trick.

"I swear on all the stars in the sky," Nick said, appearing directly in front of me out of thin air, "if you go anywhere *near* train tracks, I will be so fucking furious with you, Caspar, I will make you regret ever having the thought."

I halted abruptly and looked behind me. Blinking, I met his narrowed gaze again. "What the—how? You were—"

"Call me a stalker all you want, but I will stop you each and every time you try to hurt yourself. And if you keep pushing it, I'll take you away from here and put you someplace safe until you come to your senses."

By the look on his face, I knew he was serious. So not only did he admit to stalking me, he followed it up by basically threatening to kidnap me. Great. Just great.

"If kidnapping is the only way to get through to you, then yes. I will," Nick said, folding his arms across his chest.

Oh my God. Did I just say that shit out loud?

"No, you didn't," he replied, arching a blond brow as if to drive home the point.

"Can you...?" Read minds?

"Yes, I can."

Fuck!

I took a step backward, eyeing him with a new wariness. Maybe I shouldn't have been so blunt with him. Maybe if I'd been a little nicer he wouldn't be looking at me like he was two seconds away from tying me up and carting me off to his medieval torture chamber.

As soon as I had the image in my head of dungeons and

ancient castles, the expression on Nick's face morphed from pissed to concerned. "I'm not going to hurt you. That is, quite literally, the opposite reason for me being here."

"What *are* you doing here? What do you want from me?"

He unfolded his arms slowly and held his hands out to me, palms up.

Wetting my lips, I glanced around, looking for some sign from the universe if I should trust him or not. I mean, if he wanted to kill me, he could have done it either time he caught me standing on a rusted-out railing with an eighty-foot drop. Or, you know, at *any* point I was naked or fucking asleep.

Let's go home, Caspar.

Did he just say that? Or was that from... before? Why couldn't I get this guy out of my fucking head?

His gaze followed each of my movements — the small step forward, the uncertain swallow — all the while his face remained serene, like he knew I would cave before I did.

Sliding my rough palms over his, I took another step forward. With the darkening twilight, it was almost impossible to see the color of his eyes, but it didn't stop them from sparkling like they had on Christmas Eve. It reminded me of the way the glitter shimmered inside the snow globe. Wait. Did that mean—

"I gave it to you," Nick said softly, squeezing my hands as he pulled me closer, draping my arms over his shoulders.

"You really can read minds." I exhaled sharply, too stunned to protest being dragged forward like a doll. I mean, if he could read minds, there's no telling what else he could do.

He slipped his hands around my waist, running them up and down my back. "Can we go home now? You're freezing."

Truth be told, I hadn't even paid attention to the temperature drop. I only noticed it after he said something, after I could contrast the heat of his hands with the chill in the air.

Nodding, I went to step away from him, but his hands held me in place.

"I have a faster way," he said, the corner of his luscious mouth tilting up in a smirk.

"Ok...?"

"Hold on to me." He didn't give me much time to react before he came closer, pressing his chest against mine and tightening his arms around my waist.

I hugged his neck, inhaling the scent from the curve of his shoulder. Pine trees and peppermint. My eyes drifted shut, taking solace in the comforting smell and the way he felt against me. It was like coming home — or what I imagined a home felt like.

"We're here," he whispered a second later, lifting one hand from my waist to run through my hair.

Blinking, I looked around the inside of my cabin. "You did that before, didn't you?"

He nodded, a small smile on his lips. I could tell he was proud of himself but probably trying to downplay it so he didn't freak me out. I was already on the fence with this whole "magic" thing.

"What are you?"

"A man, like you. The only difference is my family discovered magic a long time ago."

"Nope. This is a dream. I'm dreaming again. This isn't real." I exhaled a shaky breath and pulled away from him, dropping onto the edge of my bed.

Nick sat next to me, squeezing my knee. "Did you feel that?"

"Yeah."

He leaned closer, brushing his lips against my neck and sending a wave of goosebumps down my back. "Did you feel that?"

"Yeah."

Taking one of my hands in both of his, he kissed every inch of my callused palm before laying it against his cheek. "I promise you, I'm real. You're not dreaming and you're not crazy."

I dragged my hand along the side of his cheek, brushing my thumb across his lips. Hooking the point of his chin with my forefinger, I tipped his face up as I leaned forward, pressing my lips to his.

He was warm, and soft, and tasted like peppermint. It was everything I remembered. Everything I thought was a figment of my imagination from last Christmas.

Shifting forward onto my hands and knees, my lips never left his as I climbed on top of him. He sank back into the mattress, twisting his hands in my shirt and dragging it over my head. The second the fabric was gone, he was on me, kissing and caressing my skin as I settled on top of him again.

"You have no idea how much I've missed you," he said, seizing my face and kissing me hard. His tongue swept across my lips and into my mouth, swirling around mine.

I groaned against his lips, as much from what he said as from the way he kissed me. I'd spent four months searching for a guy I thought I dreamed up and here he was again. I didn't have a clue what any of it meant, but I knew this time I wasn't going to let him go.

"I need you," Nick whispered between kisses. "I need to feel you again."

"Oh, fuck, I need that too." It was true — a flash of want and vulnerability and desperation all rolled into one. The feelings I tried to keep at bay were unleashed, tied directly to the man in my arms. I didn't know how he did it, but Nick made the impossible *seem* possible. "But I need to shower first."

"No, you don't."

"No, I really do."

"I don't want to waste a single second with you."

"Then come with me." As much as it pained me, I pushed away from him and got to my feet, holding a hand out to him.

I swore his cheeks flushed as he slipped his hand into mine and let me haul him to his feet. Another glimpse of the same innocence as last time, an authenticity I wasn't used to seeing in anyone. It was disarming. Not to mention cute as hell.

"I've missed you every day," I said, raking my hands through his silky hair and pulling him against me. Crushing my mouth to his, I tried to take as many kisses as I could, collect all his whimpers and moans, as if it could turn back the clock.

Nick broke away, panting, and pressed his forehead to mine. "Can we please skip the shower?"

"No." I kissed him quickly and led him into the bathroom.

Nick

CHAPTER FOUR

It wasn't the same shower I'd first seen Caspar in, but it still sent a shiver down my spine. Earlier, on his bed, he thought *I* was *his* dream come true. He had no idea it was actually the opposite — he was the dream, the fantasy-turned-reality.

Standing in front of him in a steamy shower, a woody fragrance filling up the air, I let myself marvel at him. I dragged my hands along his sculpted body, chasing the water and the suds as they ran down the ridges of his skin. I knew the object of this was to get clean, but all I wanted to do was dirty him up again.

Letting my hand drift between us, I stroked his cock, coaxing it from its semi-hard state back to being hard as a rock. He thrust into my palm at the same time he captured my mouth with his, sucking on my lower lip before ultimately biting it.

The sharp sting drew a moan out of me and I tightened my grip on his shaft.

He didn't let up the attack on my mouth. One hand slipped through my wet hair, tangling at the back so he could direct me into whatever position he wanted. Just like before, I was more than happy to let him use me, to take what pleasure I could offer.

When we were both breathless, he let go of my hair and nosed along my jaw, kissing and biting my throat.

"I can't get enough of you," he murmured into my skin, his hands slipping and sliding up my back, down my arms, around to my ass — anywhere he could reach. "You know, I hated peppermint before you came along."

"I'm not a candy cane," I murmured, even as I tipped my head back to expose more of myself to his ravenous attention.

"You taste like one."

"I want to know what *you* taste like." I didn't give him time to process that statement before I slid down his body and knelt before him. Gripping the base of his cock, I held it steady while I dragged the flat of my tongue along its smooth length.

His head fell back and he grabbed the curtain rod for balance. "Oh, fuck, Nick."

Sliding my hand up and down, I swirled my tongue around the crown of his dick, paying extra attention to the beads of pre-cum as they appeared. It was a taste I didn't think I'd ever grow tired of — a slight salty bitterness, like dark cacao. It was pure indulgence, meant to be savored over a long period of time. And that's exactly what I'd do if he let me.

Sucking more of him into my mouth, I relaxed my throat and went as deep as I could to get as much of his taste as possible.

A shiver rippled through him and he groaned, threading his fingers through the top of my hair. "Just like that."

I couldn't help but moan around his dick, pleased with myself that he was happy thus far. Except, when I did, he gasped and thrust deeper into my mouth.

"Fuck," he breathed, his hips moving in tiny, aborted thrusts, like he couldn't help himself.

I let my gaze drift upward, meeting his. Sucking hard, I ran my tongue along the ridge underneath the head of his cock, committing his expression to memory. I wanted him to look at me like that forever, with barely-contained lust, like he was seconds away from shoving me against the wall and having his way with me.

"Oh my God. You look so fucking hot like this."

Pulling myself off his dick completely, I kept stroking it, twisting around the head every now and again, making sure to vary the technique. "It's because you taste so good. I could do this all night."

"Fuck, Nick." He seized my arms and yanked me to my feet. Kissing me roughly, his tongue invaded my mouth, sweeping as far as he could go and leaving me dizzy. With his arms wrapped around me, he was the only thing keeping me upright. Our bodies pressed together so tightly even the water couldn't slip between us. "I can't wait anymore," he said between insatiable kisses, his voice rough. "I have to have you."

"Then take me. I'm yours, Caspar. I've always been yours."

Something indecipherable darted across his face. Before I could fully understand it, he was kissing me again, our cocks slipping and sliding against one another.

Since he didn't seem like he was making a move to actually get *out* of the shower, I took matters into my own hands. I held him tightly and whisked us to the bedroom. One minute we were standing in the shower, dripping wet, and the next we were laying on his bed, still mostly wet but I didn't think either of us really cared about that at the moment.

He pulled away with a furrowed brow and stole a quick glance around the room. "That's still really weird."

"You'll get used to it."

"I hope so." He kissed me again before sliding off the bed. Grabbing my hips, he pulled me across the mattress until my ass was right at the edge. Kneeling in front of me, he pushed his forearm across the backs of my thighs, tilting my hips up at an angle he must have preferred.

If this was anything like last time, I knew what was coming and I clutched the sheets in anticipation. The warm, wet stroke of his tongue swept across my hole and I couldn't help the moan that escaped me. Circling the rim, alternating between little flicks and long laps, Caspar's tongue worked me over in blissfully agonizing torture. My cock was practically dripping and even the few, rough jerks I gave it did nothing to relieve the painful throbbing.

Dragging his tongue up to my sac, Caspar kissed and licked the sensitive skin there, making me squirm even more.

"I'm begging you," I whined, unable to stop the desperate roll of my hips.

"But I haven't had this yet." He pushed my thighs apart, enveloping my cock in the hot, wet perfection of his mouth. An appreciative noise rumbled in the back of his throat and he took in even more, letting the excess saliva run down my length before he stroked the base and smeared it across my balls.

"Oh, yeah... That feels amazing." My fingers disappeared into his dark hair, twisting gently. I tried not to thrust up into his mouth, but I couldn't help it. I needed more. I was literally aching for more. There had been a cold emptiness inside of me since Christmas that only he could fill, with his dark chocolate eyes and cinnamon lips, burning and comforting at the same time.

He sucked the head of my dick one last time before letting go and leaning over to the nightstand. Coming back with a clear bottle in his hands, he flipped the cap and drizzled the contents over himself. An overwhelming smell of peppermint hit my nose, almost making my eyes water.

"What is that?" I furrowed my brow at the mischievous grin on his lips.

"It's peppermint. I really, *really* missed you."

"Did you think about me?"

"You know I did. You were all I could think about. I looked for you everywhere."

"I've always been right here," I said, trailing my fingers across his chest, over his heart.

"I'm not letting you go this time." He leaned forward and kissed me, the head of his cock pressing against my hole. He kept kissing me as he pushed past my entrance, the peppermint cooling me from the inside out as my body stretched to accept him.

A tremble rolled through me and my breath came in quicker bursts.

Caspar stilled inside of me, pressing kisses to my face, jaw, and ear.

"I'm ok," I said, caressing his cheek and giving him a small smile in the hopes of reassuring the worry running through his head. "I want it rough, but maybe a warm-up first?"

"Whatever you want. Just tell me."

I scooted back on my elbows and threw a pointed glance at the bed beside me. "Come lay down."

He slid out of me carefully and laid in the spot I indicated. As soon as he was in position, I shifted onto his lap. He must have realized what I wanted because he held his cock in place for me while resting his other hand on my waist to provide some support.

Sinking down slowly, I gasped and gritted my teeth. The peppermint effect was starting to wear off and now I felt him in his entirety, doing exactly what I wanted — filling me up and chasing away that cold emptiness.

Concern lined his face as he gazed up at me, both hands

resting on my hips. He didn't move at all, except for the rise and fall of his chest.

"This is how you like it, right? I mean, one of the ways?" I asked, hating that images of him and Ryan popped into my head. Rolling my hips, I rocked just a bit, testing out the new position.

"I like anything when it comes to you." Other than caressing my chest and abs with his fingertips, he still didn't move beneath me.

Lifting myself up a little at a time, I sank back down and swiveled my hips against his to take him as deep as I could. It must have been ok from the way he bit his lips and the muscles in his chest tightened beneath my hands.

As soon as I found my rhythm, I moved faster, rocking up and down on his cock until my own was slapping against his abdomen, leaving evidence of my arousal all over his skin in slippery strands.

Gripping me by the hips, he finally allowed himself to move and thrust upward right as I came down. The combined momentum sent a jolt through me. Groaning, I forced my eyes open, taking in his devilish smirk.

"Do it again," I breathed, leaning back and propping myself on his thighs to give myself a more stable foundation.

Caspar's hands tightened on me a second before he slammed in again. I squeaked in surprise, but it quickly faded to a sigh and then more moaning when he kept up the pace. Now I was the one motionless, balancing above him as he fucked into me from underneath.

"This isn't working for me," he said, right before his hands shifted up my waist and encircled my ribcage.

In the time it took me to register what he said, he'd withdrawn from inside of me and threw me backward to the opposite side of the bed. Any fear of rejection was erased the moment he crawled on top of me and wedged himself between my thighs.

"I need to kiss you," he whispered, before doing just that. "I can't kiss you when you're on top of me."

"I told you, you can do whatever you want to me."

"I plan to." He licked across my lips before grinning and scooting back, resting on his heels. Grabbing the bottle of peppermint again, he squirted more into his palm. I thought he was going to slide into me again, but he went back to sucking and licking my cock. Something still pressed against me, seeking entrance. With the fresh layer of lubrication, it didn't take much for two of his fingers to slip inside.

Giving one final kiss to my cock, he worked his way up my body to my mouth, one kiss and bite at a time, all while his fingers worked in and out. Curling along my walls, they grazed the spot that was guaranteed to make me moan as shivers raced up and down my spine.

His tongue and his fingers slid in and out of me, stroking and caressing. It wasn't long before he turned me into a writhing, panting mess and I was sure I was on the verge of hyperventilating.

"Please," I breathed, bucking against his hand, trying to direct his fingers where I wanted. "Fuck me again."

"But then it'll be game over. I'm already about to blow just from hearing you moan."

"I don't care. I need you inside me."

Pressing his lips to mine, he pulled away with a wolfish gleam in his eye and positioned himself at my hole again. He didn't even need to hold his dick steady; as soon as he nudged against my rim, he sank inside with ease. We each let out a contented groan as our bodies joined together perfectly.

Grasping my thighs, Caspar rocked his hips and thrust in again. I tried to keep my eyes open, to watch the dark intensity on his face, but every time his dick slid along that bundle of nerves, my eyes sank closed. He was right though — it was about to be game over for both of us. I didn't care. We had all night to pleasure each other. All of eternity if I had my way.

Caspar kept up the pace, pistoning in and out, using his hold on my thighs as leverage while he drove into me. I tried to touch myself, but my dick was so hard it was throbbing and I was afraid any additional stimulation would push me into an orgasm too quickly. It was inevitable, but I wanted to wait for him, to make the most of our time together.

"I'm going to fucking come," Caspar said. His voice was hoarse, but it was music to my ears.

"Fuck yes. Do it. I need to feel it."

He gave a short cry and slammed into me again. His hips jerked against mine, his cock pulsating deep inside me like the last time.

Seizing the back of my head, he kissed me roughly, all teeth and tongue and a renewed sense of urgency. We swallowed each other's moans, exchanging breath as if we were one, joined in every possible way.

I fisted my cock and jerked myself quickly, chasing the release he'd been expertly pushing me toward.

As soon as his teeth sank into my lower lip, stars burst behind my eyelids and lightning raced down my spine. The pressure in my lower abdomen exploded in spurt after spurt. Four months — no, a *lifetime* — of desire and pure, primal need shot between us, coating us both.

Another tremble wracked my body as I lay there, chest heaving, trying to remind myself that this was real and not my own wet dream in the making. Throughout the whole of my fantastical life, Caspar was the only thing that was truly magic and he didn't even know it.

Caspar slumped on top of me, burying his face in the side of my neck. "You're fucking incredible."

"I'm nothing without you."

Picking up his head, a brief smile curved his lips before he pressed them to mine in a kiss so tender a surge of indescribable emotions welled inside of me.

"Don't leave this time," he whispered, brushing his nose against mine, his dark eyes shining with sincerity — and worry.

"I won't."

A HEAVY KNOCK SOUNDED AT THE DOOR, JARRING ME out of a deep, satiated slumber. Caspar sat up behind me, pressing the heel of his hand into one eye and squinting at the clock on the mantel.

"What time is it?" he asked, turning his gaze to me. A soft, sleepy smile stretched across his face. "You're still here."

"Your friend Ryan is at the door," I said, trying not to sound as bitter as I was. I knew I didn't have a right to be, but I didn't care about morality when it came to Caspar.

"Fuck." Caspar looked around quickly and hopped out of bed. He grabbed a pair of pajama pants out of the dresser and dragged them on as Ryan knocked again, even louder.

He cleared his throat and opened the door, promptly leaning against it. "What's up?"

"I texted. You didn't answer," Ryan said from the doorway.

"Yeah, I was in the middle of something."

"Oh. Well, can I come in?"

"It's not a good time for me."

"Sounds like someone is here with you."

"As a matter of fact—"

A painful prickling erupted across my skin, drowning out

the rest of Caspar's response. The world around me swirled with colors and I screamed, trying to dig my nails into Caspar's metal bed frame like claws.

"No! You can't do this!" I shouted at the sparkling dots of color, holding on with all the strength I had.

It wasn't enough.

I slammed into the frozen ground, knocking all the wind out of me. Coughing and sucking in a ragged breath, I pushed myself into a sitting position and glared at the shiny black boots planted in front of me. Following them up vertically, I skipped past the crimson pants, the white shirt, and locked eyes with my father.

"I cannot believe you," Father said, throwing a long, fur-lined coat at me. "Cover yourself before someone sees you like this."

Seething, I yanked the coat over my naked body and got to my feet. "You had *no* right!"

"*You* have no right!" Father shouted back, his lips twisting beneath his trimmed, white beard. "Sixteen hundred years of tradition and you want to throw it all away! And for what?"

I opened my mouth for a rebuttal, but he kept going.

"Aside from the fact he is a *non*believer, he is a *he*! You are meant to marry, have children, and carry on this tradition, Nicholas! It is your birthright!"

"I don't fucking want it!" I snarled. "Let Noel have it all! The kingdom, the tradition, the fucking impossible standards *you* set for us! I don't want any of it! I'd rather melt this entire place to the ground than be a part of *your* legacy!"

"How dare you! You, of all people, will not speak to me like that. I am your father and as such I forbid you from seeing that mortal anymore."

"You can't do that!" I shouted, my hands clenching into fists at my sides.

"Can't I?" he thundered back, narrowing the distance

between us and leaning in so close we were only inches apart. "As of this moment, you're forbidden from leaving the castle. If you so much as step one foot outside its walls, I swear on all that is holy, I'll do more than blacklist that mortal."

Fury, hot and all-consuming, raged inside of me. "You'd sacrifice his soul just to punish me?! How could you?!"

"I will not let you destroy everything this family has built. Do not push me on this, Nicholas. You will *not* like the consequences."

His threat hung around me like heavy chains, crushing my soul and strangling any thought of fighting back. I could barely breathe beneath the weight of it all, let alone speak at full volume. "I hate you."

"We all make sacrifices for the greater good. In time you'll learn this was for the best." He sniffed and stomped off the way he came, leaving me alone in the middle of a silent, snow-covered forest, lost in a sea of evergreens. I crumpled where I stood as a sob tore out of me, echoing through the frozen winterland.

Caspar

CHAPTER FIVE

For the first time in a long time, I was content. Dare I say happy? My arm tightened around Nick and I slid my leg between his, pushing his thighs apart so I could contour myself to him even more. Kissing the back of his neck as he slept, I inhaled his scent again and again. It was everything I remembered — everything I'd been missing and didn't even realize. The pine, the peppermint, a clean crispness that reminded me of fresh snow. And yet, holding him, I was filled with a comforting warmth, like I was home. Could people be a place? People say "Home is where the heart is," so maybe they could.

I fell asleep to that thought, picturing Nick in wintertime. What would he do, for instance, if I chucked a snowball at him while we shoveled the driveway? Would we play rock, paper, scissors to see who had to climb out of bed in the middle of the night to add more logs to the fireplace or just be adults and take turns? If I kissed him right after he drank hot chocolate, would I still taste the mint flavor on his skin?

All those thoughts were disrupted by a banging on the door. Groaning, I sat up and rubbed a hand over my face, trying to make out the time on the clock since I had no idea where my cell phone was.

"What time is it?" I asked out loud, finally remembering in my half-consciousness that I was talking to Nick. The *real* Nick, not the voice that floated around in my head. The flesh and blood version of him was laying right next to me, his face scrunched in sleepy irritation. I couldn't help but smile like an idiot and then proceed to say the dumbest thing ever. "You're still here."

"Your friend Ryan is at the door," he replied flatly.

"Fuck."

That "Fuck" covered more than one problem.

Firstly, Nick knew about Ryan. Considering he had some weird mystical abilities we hadn't quite discussed yet, I figured it was probably part of the package.

Secondly, Nick was *pissed* about Ryan. I might have been half-asleep but I didn't miss the way his body went rigid and his lips formed a hard line.

And thirdly, Ryan was here, after dark, which only meant one thing. So this was bound to get awkward. We weren't official or exclusive or anything other than fuck buddies, but that wasn't for lack of trying on his part. Hopefully I could shoo him out of here and we could "break up" some other day.

Yanking on a pair of pajamas on the way to the door, I cleared my throat and exhaled sharply in preparation of the potential fallout to come.

Cracking open the door, I braced my arm against the frame and leaned on the knob, trying to block Ryan's view of the inside as much as possible. "What's up?"

Ryan frowned at me, his gaze immediately trying to flick past my shoulder. "I texted. You didn't answer."

I shifted to the side, my grip tightening on the door handle. "Yeah, I was in the middle of something."

"Oh." He blinked once, his blue eyes narrowed. He gave me a moment before adding, "Well, can I come in?"

Wincing, I tried to look as apologetic as possible. "It's not a good time for me..."

"Sounds like someone is here with you."

"As a matter of fact, yeah. Look, it was kind of out of the blue. Ok? I didn't, like, *plan* it."

Ryan nodded, forcing a smile to his face. "Yeah, no I get it. Have a... good night." He looked like he wanted to say something else, but he swallowed the words and turned, retreating down the front walkway to his car.

I closed the door slowly and let out a long exhale. That went over better than I thought. I mean, I hadn't lied, but I still felt like an ass. Mostly because Ryan was a good guy. He deserved more than me. Nick deserved more than me, too, but I couldn't help the preternatural pull I felt toward him. I think it was safe to say it was mutual, which assuaged my guilt for being a selfish asshole.

"Sorry about that," I said, spinning on the ball of my foot. Blinking, I stopped dead in my tracks.

The bed was empty.

"Nick?"

There was no response.

Frowning, I headed for the bathroom, but he wasn't there either.

"Nick?"

Where the fuck was he? There was only one door in or out of the cabin and considering I could pretty much see every corner of it from where I was standing, it's not like he could be hiding somewhere.

"Nick!"

Panic crept along my spine, cold tendrils snaking along my torso and squeezing mercilessly. Shaking my head, I ran to the door and shoved my feet into boots before sprinting down the driveway.

I didn't stop sprinting until I reached the bridge. "Nick!"

Whirling in a circle, I searched the moonlit landscape for him, but he was gone. He was fucking *gone*.

"No, not again..." I couldn't stop my lower lip from quivering. Wrapping my arms around myself, I rubbed them briskly, trying in vain to bring some semblance of warmth back to my skin.

Walking to the railing, I stared out over the winding black water. Cupping my hands around my mouth, I screamed his name into the night until the only sound I could make was a scratchy squeak.

My voice left me, just like he did.

Nick

CHAPTER SIX

Thousands of miles away, on another plane of existence, I heard my name being screamed into the wind and it shattered what was left of my broken heart.

Cradling the snow globe in my hands, I watched Caspar run to the bridge as soon as he realized I was gone. Then it was me screaming at him.

"Don't you dare! Caspar! Don't!"

I don't know if he actually heard me, but he slumped against the railing before sliding to the ground. His shoulders shook and he covered his face with one hand.

"I'm sorry," I whispered, stroking the cold glass like the sensation would somehow pass through and reach him. "I'm *so* sorry. I didn't want to leave you."

And so, that's how I spent my days, watching Caspar through a watery lens and trying not to do something stupid, like flee my icy prison and rush right back to him.

I worked in silence alongside my father, exchanged sullen glances with my brother, Noel, and avoided my mother's sympathetic gaze.

The days turned to weeks and weeks to months. In Caspar's world, spring turned to summer, and summer wilted into autumn. Meanwhile, I was trapped in a perpetual winter, in more ways than one.

Caspar fell into a similar, monotonous pattern. Most days he went through the motions like I did. Work, bridge, home. Work, bridge, home. Sometimes he'd stay there for hours, yelling, drinking, cursing my name.

One autumn night, after he plowed through another bottle of whiskey, Caspar pulled himself up on the railing and flung the empty bottle into the night sky.

"Where are you this time?" he shouted, teetering precariously on the thin bar. "Huh? Look! I'm on the railing! The one place you never want me to be!"

I squeezed the snow globe so hard I was sure it would shatter at any minute between my hands. "Caspar, you reckless fool! Don't you dare do this to me!"

"If you're out there, watching, you better come stop me!" He swung around one of the sway braces and landed on another section of the railing.

"Get down!" I snarled through my teeth. For once, I wished that shaking the snow globe would throttle him in the process, like a child with an ant farm. Maybe it would knock some sense into him.

"Not perilous enough yet?!" Caspar scurried up the rickety metal bars and hooked his leg around one of the trusses at the top of the bridge. I'd seen him do it at work, hanging on rafter beams to run wiring and whatnot. I was irritated, but not concerned. At least, I wasn't concerned until he hooked both legs over the truss and let go with his hands, hanging upside down like a bat and dangling above certain death.

I raked a hand through my hair, expelling a sharp breath. Could I make it if he fell? Was my magic fast enough? But then what? Even if I saved him from plummeting headfirst into the river, I'd condemn his soul. Someone even worse than my father would come for him and then there'd be nothing I could do.

Caspar jackknifed upward, grabbing onto the truss with his hands again. He swung his legs down, dangling from the tips of his fingers with a grimace. Between the cold and the rust, I'm sure the metal was biting into his hands. All the more reason for him to—

"Get down!" a voice shouted, but it wasn't mine.

Caspar and I both looked at the end of the bridge and the figure hurrying over.

It was Ryan.

A mixture of relief and anger twisted my insides into knots. While I appreciated that Caspar wasn't alone anymore, I was livid it was Ryan coming to his rescue and not me.

Caspar's laugh punched through my murderous thoughts. He swung his feet a little as he hung there, making no move to follow the command. "What are you doing here?"

"I was driving by," Ryan replied, his hands poised like he was ready to catch Caspar if he fell. "What are you doing? It's not safe up there."

"I know. That's why I'm *up* here."

"Well, come down! It's hard to talk to you like this."

Caspar let go with one hand. Ryan and I both yelped. A dark little chuckle echoed across the bridge. "You said come down."

"Oh my God. Not like that!"

"Why not? What's the worst that can happen?"

"Just *please* be careful," Ryan said, covering his mouth with both hands pressed together, like he was praying.

Sighing, Caspar reached up and grabbed the lip of the truss again. He swung his legs back and forth a few times, building up the momentum before he let go on a forward swing. Landing in a crouch in the middle of the bridge, he stood slowly and dusted his hands off.

I closed my eyes and exhaled a breath, willing my heart to return to a normal pace. Damn him! Damn him for taking unnecessary risks.

When I opened my eyes again, I immediately wished I hadn't.

Caspar had Ryan caged against the railing, his tongue firmly in Ryan's mouth while Ryan's hands groped every part of Caspar not covered by his canvas jacket.

"Caspar, don't," I hissed, shaking my head. At him, at myself, at the stupid fucking rule that kept us apart. It should have been *me* down there, not Ryan. Not anyone. Just me and Caspar. But once again, I was *here* and he was *there*.

Now, because of some ancient canon established by our ancestors, I had to stand by and watch another man move in on the only person I'd ever cared about — the only one who had ever cared about me.

Ryan got on his knees and pulled Caspar's cock out of his jeans, swallowing it down without a second thought. Caspar's hips flicked and he ran both hands through Ryan's hair, glinting a pale gold in the moonlight. Ryan grabbed his ass, squeezing him so hard I could see the tiny imprint in the snow globe.

In spite of my anger, my own cock hardened and pressed against the row of buttons on my pants, desperate to be let out.

"One of these days, Caspar," I muttered, shoving the black fabric down my thighs and palming myself roughly. "You're going to pay for that little stunt on the truss."

Suddenly, Caspar grabbed Ryan's biceps and yanked him upward, kissing him roughly before sinking to his knees. He pulled Ryan's dick out and lapped along its length, stroking with his hand and sucking on the head.

"You're going to pay for that too," I growled, squeezing my shaft and thrusting into my own fist. "Because that's *my* mouth. It's not meant for him."

I was almost on the edge when Caspar stood and turned Ryan around. Stepping up behind him, Caspar kicked his feet apart and bent him over the railing. Angling Ryan's hips against him, I knew the moment Caspar sank inside him by the way his eyes screwed shut.

Their moans mingled with mine. Simply remembering how it felt when Caspar pushed inside me, staking a claim no one else would ever have, wrath and lust spun together in my blood.

"You'll pay for *all* your rashness," I said, pumping my cock in tandem with the thrusting of Caspar's hips. I could almost feel his breath on my skin, the possessiveness of each and every touch, the growls and the sighs.

I bit my lip, stifling a cry as my icy-hot release jetted onto my abdomen.

Flopping back in the pile of pillows on my bed, I exhaled a shaky breath, staring at the dark green canopy overhead.

"I'm going to find a way," I said, hefting the snow globe into view and watching as Caspar kissed Ryan goodbye and strolled down the road, his hands shoved in his pockets. "I'm going to find a way to get to you. Because, unlike you, I don't break my promises."

Caspar

CHAPTER SEVEN

uck Christmas.

F It was the constant thought I had from Thanks-giving onward. Really, from Halloween onward because goddamn Christmas kept creeping up, earlier and earlier each fucking year.

When the snow fell early in December, my disgust hit its apex.

Overnight, Coventry threw up fucking Christmas decorations on anything that stood still. Lighted garland twisted around the wrought-iron lamp posts. Windows flickered with lit candles or twinkling lights. More than one mailbox or front door was wrapped to look like a goddamn candy cane or a Christmas present. Everyone ran around acting like old friends, wishing each other "Happy Holidays" and a "Merry Christmas" even though that shit was weeks away. Never mind the fact they hadn't talked to those people in years and wouldn't until the next time they happened to run into each other.

And as those weeks progressed, the Christmas cheer in Coventry turned into Christmas anxiety. The well-wishes continued but people had that harried look in their eyes as they crowded the streets, snatching last-minute presents from shelves and dragging sobbing children up to the town gazebo to see "Santa," to ask for more shit their parents couldn't afford to buy.

Of the few that truly enjoyed Christmas, I'd bet all the money I didn't have there were five more who put on their fake smiles and carried out these stupid traditions because of peer pressure. Whether it was for their kids, their spouses, or society in general, if you responded with anything less than a Tiny Tim-level of enthusiasm people labeled you a Scrooge and gave you the side-eye for the rest of the season. The worst was when they talked about you behind your back, tut-tutting your "predicament" while you were still within earshot.

My "predicament," Susan, was none of your fucking business, so take your sugar plum danish and your peppermint mocha latte and fuck right off.

I turned up the collar on my coat and hunched my shoulders, trying to navigate the yearly Christmas gauntlet, dodging a fuck-ton of people and all their goddamn shopping bags.

A group of carolers, who clearly fell out of a Dickens novel and needed to go back, tried to serenade me as I passed. Besides the fact I hated Christmas music, I was trying not to bust my ass on the icy, snow-covered sidewalk, so *no*, I did *not* want to stop and enjoy your impromptu performance.

After successfully waving off the carolers with all five of my gloved fingers, it was time to ignore the obnoxious bell-ringers soliciting charitable donations. People didn't give a fuck any other time of year, so why was December suddenly the giving season? Other than using it as a last-minute tax write-off, it was yet another expectation people had to fulfill or look like a giant jackass.

Yanking open the door to the liquor store, I tipped my chin up at the clerk as I stamped the snow off my boots.

"We just got some more of that peppermint RumChata in," John said, pointing to the detestable display of red-and-white striped bottles. "Some Smirnoff and Schnapps over there too."

"Hard pass." I steered clear of anything minty and grabbed a bottle of Fireball.

"Yeah, I'm not a fan myself. Aggravates the heartburn."

I snorted, setting the bottle on the counter and pulling a few bills out of my wallet. "Heartburn, huh?" Funny, peppermint gave me heartburn too but it had nothing to do with fucking acid reflux.

"It's hell getting old, kid," he replied, ringing up the sale and counting out my change.

"I'm not too worried about it." I waved him off when he tried to hand me the leftover money. "Nah, keep it."

"Thanks, Caspar. Merry Christmas."

Plastering on my fake-as-fuck smile, I nodded and bolted to the door, twisting off the cap as I went. Cinnamon and whiskey scorched a path across my tongue and down my esophagus, warming me from the inside out as I returned to the wintry night.

Thankfully, people had started to clear out of the streets, giving me room to breathe for a change. I needed it after John inadvertently gave *me* a case of heartburn.

I'd successfully avoided thinking about Nick since Thanksgiving. That had been my last trip to the bridge. My last shouting match with nothing but air. If it was possible for me to hate anything more than Christmas, it was Nick.

How could he insert himself into my life — twice! — and disappear without a fucking trace? Who does that? Why bother coming around at all? Once he was gone, he should have stayed gone. I'd already convinced myself he was a dream. I was ok with that. But no. There was no way I could convince myself I was dreaming after he appeared the second time.

Especially not with that fucking snow globe sitting there, mocking me.

I promise you, I'm real.

Oh, yeah, I knew he was real because he was a fucking liar like everyone else in my life. He promised to stay and he left anyway.

As soon as I got back from wallowing at the bridge that day in April I shoved the fucking snow globe in a cabinet, forcing myself to forget about it. So of course, seven months later, I had to unearth it on Thanksgiving when I went in search of a goddamn roasting pan.

I said the hell with the turkey and carried the snow globe to the bridge to get rid of it once and for all. The glitter snowflakes sparkled in the late November sunlight, gleaming and twirling as the water sloshed around. The ice castle inside was almost translucent. It was pretty. Delicate. I couldn't wait to watch it shatter.

Stepping up to the railing, I held the globe between my hands and stared at it. Why would he give me this? I mean, who the fuck carries a snow globe around with them on a whim? He did have that whole Santa thing going on that night. And he said his family had magic. Maybe he conjured it or something. Or I was completely delusional.

I'll do whatever it takes to make it better.

Except, Nick made it worse. He made it a thousand times worse. In addition to that stupid fucking snow globe, he gave me the one thing I never wanted — hope.

When he was there, I felt like the sky was the limit. We could do anything as long as we were together. Nick saw me in a way no one else did. He saw through all of my bullshit and reached back to a version of me that hadn't been hurt time and again, promising to give that scared little kid a safe place to land. And as crazy as it was, for a few hours I believed in him. I believed Nick *would* make things better.

Retreating from the railing, I cradled the snow globe against my chest and trudged back to my cabin. Begrudgingly, I set it on the nightstand and went back to making dinner.

And I didn't think of Nick again. I didn't whisper his name in my mind. I didn't shake the snow globe and wonder where he was. I let it sit there and collect dust because I was too chicken shit to throw it out. I tried to move on — and was doing fairly well — until John had to bring it all up again with one well-meaning comment.

I cycled through everything Nick had ever said as I drove home, taking swigs of whiskey along the way. By the time I pulled into my driveway, half of the bottle was gone.

I left the truck running and ran inside to grab one thing before I got behind the wheel again. Instead of driving to the bridge, I turned north and headed for an even more remote part of Maine, deeper into the land of never-ending pine trees.

As soon as I hit the railroad tracks, I pulled off the roadway. I might have been in the middle of nowhere, but I turned west, away from the road and any potential rescuers.

My truck knocked the snow off the pine boughs as I drove alongside the tracks. Once it was sufficiently hidden from the crossing, I cut the engine but didn't get out.

I swallowed the last bit of whiskey with a grimace. The cinnamon had lost its appeal in the last quarter of the bottle, but it was better than fucking peppermint.

Throwing the empty bottle over my shoulder, I grabbed the snow globe from the passenger seat and shook it. My thoughts swirled around like little snowflakes. Every once in a while I'd get a flash of a memory or a feeling, but then it would be gone again, making it hard to tell what was real and what was just my stupid wish.

The only thing linking the shattered fragments together was Nick.

I didn't understand him. I didn't understand *anything* about him.

The two times he'd shown up were at the bridge, but I spent seven months trying to get him to reappear and he didn't. And now it was Christmas Eve again. His promised year was up. My life hadn't gotten better. It got worse.

The housing market was unstable, which meant construction jobs were few and far between. Money was always tight but in a season dedicated to spending, it was even more obvious. It wasn't the "thought" that counted anymore, it was how big the price tag was. For someone who had nothing, or next to nothing, it was another kick when you were already down.

Then again, you had to have people in your life to even bother worrying about Christmas presents. Other than co-workers and my weekly trip to see John at Coventry Liquors, I didn't associate with anyone. Even Ryan wasn't in the picture anymore. After months of a mutually-beneficial arrangement, he'd gone and fallen in love with some guy down in Farmington. Not that I could blame him. He finally saw the writing on the wall as far as I was concerned. The most I could do for him was help him pack his apartment, load the moving van, and send him on his way with a farewell fuck.

In case you weren't feeling lonely enough with all of the feel-good movies and commercials being shoved down your throat every time you turned around, taking a gander through pretty much any window was guaranteed to remind you how much this holiday fucking sucked.

Inside all the perfectly decorated houses, you could look in as families gathered and carried out their annual traditions. Kids were excited to finally get all their toys and parents were relieved it was finally over. The year had been building to this — this holiday meant for families and families alone. Single people were, by default, tag-alongs; add-ons to the dinner table, receivers of the generic gifts kept on standby, and the butt of family ribbing about their lack of a partner.

I was fucking over it.

It was funny how my job was to literally build things for people and yet my own life was falling apart. Once again, not funny "ha ha" just funny as in "fucking pathetic."

Since I'd established I was a pussy at the bridge and didn't have the balls to actually jump, I had to go with another alternative.

Climbing out of the truck, I trudged up the rocky right of way to the railroad tracks. The snow globe weighed a thousand pounds. It was like lugging a boulder up there. I should have left the fucking thing in the truck, or chucked it into the river like my first plan was. I don't even know why I brought the fucking thing with me.

At the top of the tracks, I turned in a slow circle, taking in the vastness around me. Pale blue moonlight shone over the landscape. Nothing but trees and snow for miles. There wasn't a single Christmas light to be seen anywhere. At least, not that I could tell with my gaze going in and out of focus.

The world spun, sloshing the whiskey around inside of me. I sank into a crouch slowly but ended up teetering and landing on my ass.

"Shit." I groaned and laid back, resting my head over the rail. I'd probably regret it in a minute, but for the time being I appreciated the freezing metal cooling the back of my neck. Stretching my legs out over the other rail, I planted my boots on the ground and bent my knees, setting the stupid snow globe on my lap.

The glitter twinkled back at me. It fucking *twinkled*. Either my drunken imagination was officially off the rails (ha, pun intended) or it was a memory trying to bust through the cinnamon blockade.

No matter how I tried to ignore those sparkling, iridescent

colors, all I could think about were Nick's eyes. They glinted the same way — in moonlight, in firelight, it didn't matter. I'd never seen anything like it, except now, staring into the snow globe.

And then suddenly those deep blue eyes actually stared back at me from inside the snow globe.

"I wish you were here," I muttered with a scowl before laughing because I was a fucking idiot, sitting in the middle of nowhere talking to a goddamn decoration. "I hate you, and yet I wish you were here. How sad is that? I'd rather be with you than anyone else and I don't even fucking know you. Except... I thought I did."

You do.

"Oh, God. Don't start that shit again." I scrubbed a hand over my face before glaring at the snow globe and the illusion of Nick's face. "Don't act like we're something when we're not. You were a fucking possibility and that's it. A possibility that didn't pan out. So you don't get to Monday-morning quarterback my ass anymore."

Caspar...

Phantom Nick looked so sad, but ask me if I cared.

"Shut up. I should have told you to fuck off last year. Then I wouldn't be in this mess because I'd be fucking gone. Do you hear me? Gone! Just like you are! Why make me stay? Why make me get down if you were just going to up and leave? Huh? Are you some sick, sadistic fuck who likes to go around ruining people's lives?"

The Nick in the globe was pissed. His jaw clenched so hard I could see it through all the snowflakes swirling around. Good. Let him be pissed because *I* was pissed. Maybe it was time for him to feel what I felt. Maybe it was time for him to live without me. If he even bothered coming back to Coventry.

Don't you dare.

A heavy vibration rumbled through my chest. Laughter, along with the telltale clacking of an oncoming train. Out here, in the middle of nowhere, I highly doubted the engineer would even see me. The train didn't show any signs of stopping. There was no whistle. No shrieking of the brakes. Just the steady reverberation of metal wheels gliding along.

Snowflakes glittered on Nick's face, melting in streaks down his skin like tears.

Off in the distance, I could make out the sound of a church bell pealing, announcing midnight mass. I imagined people were snug inside their old stone churches, decked out in garland and candles and smelling of frankincense. I wasn't religious, but it was still a pretty thought.

I hugged the snow globe to my chest and closed my eyes with a sigh. "Merry Christmas, Nick."

Nick

CHAPTER EIGHT

Acouple of quiet knocks sounded against my bedroom
door before it creaked open. I didn't bother rolling
over to see who it was. I didn't care. I didn't care it
was Christmas Eve. I didn't care that Father had been shouting
so loud I could hear him all the way up here. I didn't care
about anything anymore. And why should I? Everything I
cared about didn't matter to him, so I wasn't going to trouble
myself trying to pretend anymore.

The bed dipped down behind me.

"Nick?" It was Noel.

"Go away."

"You have to come down. Father is getting ready to leave."

"I don't care."

He sighed. "You're not helping yourself, you know. By
continuing to fight him, all you're doing is bringing attention
to... that guy."

I bristled, my jaw clenching in preparation of yet another
shouting match. So far, Noel hadn't weighed in on the situa-
tion. Now, after months of silence, if he came out on Father's
side of the argument? I might actually throw him out the

window. "Caspar has already been blacklisted. As long as I stay away from him, that's the worst of it."

"Is it?"

Sitting up slowly, I turned and faced my brother with a narrowed gaze. "What have you heard?"

Noel blinked solemnly, his emerald eyes darting to the snow globe laying next to me. "If you don't come around on your own by the new year, Father is selecting a wife on your behalf. Then you'll be married during the Feast of the Epiphany."

The bottom fell out of my stomach, along with my heart. My mouth went dry and my eyes widened. "What?!"

He nodded, swallowing thickly. "I'm so sorry, Nick. Mother tried to talk to him... but he won't be swayed."

Two weeks. *Less* than two weeks, actually, and my life would be utterly destroyed. It was hard enough being separated from Caspar, watching him move through his day-to-day life and sink deeper into despondency. And then to be thrust into a marriage I wanted *no* part of, with a person I didn't know, to carry on meaningless traditions I wanted nothing to do with? It was unfathomable.

Noel touched my shoulder and drifted out of the room, closing the door behind him.

Squeezing my eyes shut, I laid down again, curling around the snow globe. Tears, a mixture of anger and helplessness, splattered on the curved glass. Everyone saw my father as this benevolent being who labored for the good of the world. What they didn't know was it was all a lie. The image our family presented was nothing but a thin veneer of happiness, masking the fissures and jagged edges beneath. As long as people were dazzled by the outward appearance, there was no reason to dig any deeper, to see the darkness and misery behind the glittering Christmas lights.

I don't know when I fell asleep, but when I woke it was

dark. It wasn't the darkness that woke me. It was the shimmery silver light dancing behind my eyelids.

Blinking, I sat up with a gasp and hauled the snow globe closer. It was Caspar! He was staring right at me, his eyes black and shining in the moonlight. He wasn't at the bridge, nor was he at home. Point of fact, I didn't know *where* he was. In all the years I'd watched him, I'd never seen him come to this spot.

"I wish you were here," he said, gritting his teeth a second before he laughed. "I hate you, and yet I wish you were here. How sad is that? I'd rather be with you than anyone else and I don't even fucking know you. Except... I thought I did."

"You do! You do know me!" I replied quickly, all but shouting at the glass in the hopes my voice reached him.

"Oh, God. Don't start that shit again."

He heard me! I don't know how, but he heard me! Caspar, a mere mortal, had somehow tapped into the magic. If that wasn't a sign we were meant to be together, I didn't know what was.

I gripped the snow globe, but Caspar kept talking, the corners of his eyes tightening to match the scowl on his lips.

"Don't act like we're something when we're not. You were a fucking possibility and that's it. A possibility that didn't pan out. So you don't get to Monday-morning quarterback my ass anymore."

"Caspar..." I sighed, caressing the cold glass. "Please don't say that..."

"Shut up," he snapped. "I should have told you to fuck off last year. Then I wouldn't be in this mess because I'd be fucking gone. Do you hear me? Gone! Just like you are! Why make me stay? Why make me get down if you were just going to up and leave? Huh? Are you some sick, sadistic fuck who likes to go around ruining people's lives?"

Each word out of his mouth was like a knife to my heart,

but the more he talked, the more my molars ground together. None of this was my choice! Didn't he see that? I risked it all for him and if my Father had his way, then it was all for nothing! Caspar wasn't the only one hurting. I wished there was a way I could make him see that, to let him know I was still with him even though we were apart.

A train ought to do the trick.

A what?! Did I just hear him correctly?

Staring at the area around him, I spied the dark tracks in the snow. He was lying right in the middle of them!

I was on my feet now, hovering over the snow globe and shouting at the top of my lungs. I didn't care who heard me. White-hot fury burned me from the inside out. Tears of anger and frustration spilled out until his face was nothing but a blur in the globe. "Don't you dare! Caspar! Move! Now!"

The inside of the globe dimmed, swallowed by darkness.

All I could hear was a faint "Merry Christmas, Nick" before I let out a primal yell.

At that moment, I saw nothing but Caspar — thought of nothing but Caspar. Consequences be damned.

I smashed the snow globe at my feet as hard as I could. Water and crystals shattered, spraying across the floor in flashes of blues and whites and silvers.

The colors swirled around me and the familiar tingling raced across my skin.

In a second that lasted an eternity, I materialized on the tracks.

A train whistle pierced the quiet night. The brakes shrieked in protest, sparks flying along the rails.

And there was Caspar, right in the path of danger.

"Nick?" He stared up at me with wide eyes, blinking hard.

Throwing myself on top of Caspar, I wrenched the snow globe out of his hands and flung it toward the oncoming train. It shattered beneath a wheel, rupturing with another burst of blue and silver light. I squeezed my eyes shut and clung to him, thinking only of getting him home as the train screeched closer.

We landed hard on the floor of his cabin with a grunt, the air rushing out of both of us. It wasn't my best landing, but it did the trick.

As soon as I got my bearings, I pushed myself into a sitting position, straddling Caspar's lap. Instead of being relieved, I was furious. "You asshole! What do you think you were doing?! Did you forget what I told you?! Was that really an attempt to end your life or did you pull that little stunt just to get me down here again?!"

"Fuck you, Nick! You don't get to pop into my life and pass judgment! And get the fuck off of me!" He bucked his hips and tossed me to the side.

I grabbed onto his jacket and pulled him with me. Pushing off the floor the second I landed, I shoved him off, rolling with him so I came out on top again. Twisting my hands in his jacket, I pinned him to the floor, eyes narrowed. "I warned you — if you went anywhere *near* a train, I would make you regret it. And I'm going to make good on that promise."

"What are you going to do? Leave me again?" he shot back, eyes narrowed with anger. "There's the door! Don't let it hit you on the way out!"

Glaring, I hauled him to his feet and shoved him onto the bed.

He sprawled on his back, completely bereft of his clothing. A length of red velvet ribbon appeared, cinching his wrists to the metal headboard while another secured his ankles to the opposite end.

"What the fuck?!" His dark eyes flashed and he yanked on the ribbon. "Untie me!"

"No," I replied with a bitter smile, swaggering over to the bed and kneeling next to him on the mattress. "Since you seem intent on hurting yourself no matter what I have to say, I think it's time we come to an understanding."

"Oh yeah? What's that?"

"If anyone's going to hurt you, it's going to be me." To emphasize my point, I slapped my open palm on his chest.

He sucked in a breath through his teeth, my handprint blossoming on his skin. "You don't have the balls."

I leaned forward, palming his testicles and tugging on them until his hips jerked. "Don't I?"

"You better hope I don't get out of this fucking thing." He yanked against the ribbon again, the muscles in his arms and shoulders straining.

"Keep it up and I'll leave you tied up like this until spring. Point of fact, I think you've done enough talking for one night. It's time for you to listen." Scooting up the mattress, I twirled a candy cane between my fingers, arching an eyebrow at him. "Open."

"I hate peppermint," he growled.

"That's a lie and we both know it." I leaned forward and grabbed his jaw, squeezing until he did as he was instructed. Positioning the candy cane horizontally between his teeth, I gave him another fleeting smile. "Bite down, but not too hard or you'll break it. Then I'll *really* have to punish you."

He clamped down with a huff, glaring at me.

"Now that I have your undivided attention, let's clear some things up. Shall we?" I ran my fingertips down his sternum, tracing the valley through his abs, and along the length of his cock. It twitched beneath my hand, betraying its master with the movement and the fact it was starting to get hard.

Smiling to myself, I continued stroking him. Not just his cock, but all of his skin. His thighs, his stomach, back up to his arms. I wanted him to feel me everywhere in his drunken stupor, to know I was there and he was mine. From now on, I was the only one who would get to touch him like this.

"You're under the impression that my leaving was voluntary," I said, dragging my nails across his chest lightly before slapping his pec again.

He groaned, a wince darting across his face before his dark eyes returned to mine, tracking my movements. They widened when a thick, white candle appeared in my hand, its flame flickering as I brought it closer to his body.

"It *wasn't* voluntary," I continued, rubbing his reddened skin with my free hand. "I left because of my father. You don't know him, personally speaking, but rest assured he knows you." I tipped the candle, letting the hot wax drizzle over his abdomen.

Caspar hissed around the candy cane. His abs tightened and he pushed his hips down into the mattress in an attempt to squirm away from me.

I slid off the bed, circling to the other side as I spoke. "See, I've known about you for most of my life. I've watched you grow up, practically alongside me. I saw the hell you lived in. The fights you got into. The things you stole. The stuff you broke. I saw it all. Stalker, as you say? Maybe."

His chest rose and fell quicker, his gaze darting between the hand stroking his cock and the hand holding the candle.

"Or *maybe* I've been in love with you for as long as I can remember? When I look at you, I see someone fighting for their place in this world. I see someone like me, someone who is just waiting and hoping that someday *someone* will see their true worth. Guess what? I see you like no one else ever will, and I love every part of you. So the thought of you harming yourself — harming the person *I* love? Unacceptable, Caspar."

His face had softened somewhat while I spoke, but my final statement renewed the wariness in his eyes. He followed my hand as I stroked the inside of his thigh and let my fingers drift over to his cock again.

I squeezed his hard shaft at the same time I dripped another stripe of wax across his stomach.

The candy cane cracked between his teeth, his body twisting and jerking against the ribbons.

"I wouldn't break that candy if I were you," I said, setting the candle to the side. "Otherwise I'm going to have to find something else to put in your mouth to keep you from interrupting. And I'll make sure it's not pleasant."

Seething, he rolled the candy cane in his mouth, like a horse toying with a bit, trying to find a more comfortable position to hold it.

"Now, I know what you're probably thinking," I said, pulling my shirt off and tossing it to the side before slipping out of my pants. I waved away the ribbon from his ankles so I could insert myself between his legs. "This is a lot to take in. You've only seen me twice. Now three times. I realize my feelings for you run deeper than yours for me. I'm sure it will take you some time to process all of this. But I'm not going anywhere, Caspar. I've given up *everything* to be here right now. To be with *you*. I hope you understand that."

Kneeling between his legs, I ran both hands up the inside of his thighs, caressing along his length and down to his sac, keeping my touch featherlight. I couldn't help but notice he shifted his hips now and again whenever my hands went by, trying to make contact between his hard-on and whatever part of me he could.

I might have still been angry with him for his recklessness, but my desperation outweighed it. I needed him to understand how serious I was. To help make that happen, I lowered my voice and looked up at him, holding his suspicious gaze. "You think the world filled you with hate, but it didn't. It filled you with loneliness. A need to connect, to be understood. And *I* do. I feel the same way you do. I may have been surrounded by a family, but that doesn't mean they know the real me or accept me for who I am. Was I beaten and starved as a child? No. But neglect cuts just as deep. To *want* to belong more than anything? And yet you constantly find yourself on the outside looking in."

I crawled on top of him slowly, my gaze fixed on his as I made my way up his body. Hooking a finger around the end of the candy cane, I slid it out of his mouth and tossed it aside. "You see? You *do* know me, without even realizing it. We're two sides of the same coin, Caspar."

Caspar licked his lips and rubbed them together. For a minute I felt bad about essentially gagging him, but I really needed him to hear me and it was the only thing I could think of in the heat of the moment.

I was afraid he wasn't going to speak at all, even with the candy cane gone, but he finally cleared his throat softly. "You know this is fucked up, right? Everything you just said. People don't *say* shit like that. Not out loud, anyway."

"Maybe they should. Maybe if people were more honest, the world wouldn't be the way it is."

"So is that your defense? You're a psycho stalker but it's ok because you're being upfront about it?"

I considered it for a minute before nodding. "Yeah. Pretty much. I also did say I gave up everything for you. So that has to count for something. Right?"

"I might be an asshole, but you're definitely crazy. Like, a whole level of batshit I didn't know was possible." He didn't smile, but he didn't say it with any venom in his voice either. From the whirlwind of his thoughts, I got the impression he wasn't mad anymore. The whiskey might have been muddling his ability to think clearly, but when it came to me, there wasn't any hatred in his heart.

"Not crazy-crazy, just crazy about *you*," I tossed back with a smirk as I scooted back down his body. Settling between his thighs, I spread them open even wider, giving myself more room.

"Nick?"

"Hmm?" I glanced up as I licked him from root to tip and came back down, swallowing him whole.

His eyelids drifted shut for a moment before he blinked them open again. Pulling on the ribbon a couple of times, he stopped after a second and spread his hands as far as he could. "Aren't you forgetting something?"

I hummed around his dick, indicating a *No,* and continued sliding my mouth up and down.

"You have to untie me," he whined.

Popping off the end, I chuckled. "I don't *have* to do anything." Conjuring a mug of hot chocolate and an ice cube, I waggled my brows at him.

"Wait. What is that?" He craned his neck to try and see what I had. "What are you doing?"

"Don't move or you'll make a mess."

"Don't what? Why—Fuck!"

With the ice cube resting on my tongue, I took him into my mouth again, sucking and swirling the ice around the head of his cock.

His thighs trembled and he exhaled a shaky breath. "Nick!"

Giving him a reprieve, I spit out the ice cube and drank some of the hot chocolate. As soon as I swallowed the liquid, my mouth was back on him, warming the areas I'd shocked with cold. I kept at it, alternating between the hot and cold and applying the drastic temperature changes to different parts of his anatomy.

He sighed, his hips rolling to try and get his cock in deeper each time my mouth was extra-hot. "What are you doing to me?"

"You've been *very* naughty while I've been gone," I said,

setting the empty mug aside and picking up another chunk of ice. "I am *not* happy with you."

"If you want me to make you happy, don't put that ice anywhere near my dick again. While you're at it, you should untie me. I'm not much good to you like this."

"You're perfect the way you are. And don't worry. This isn't for your dick anymore." I dragged the ice up his stomach to his chest, running it across each nipple and leaving wet trails on his skin. Scraping the chunks of wax off his stomach, I soothed the red stripes beneath with the ice.

Once he was clean, I shifted further south with the ice, giving him a devilish grin as it dipped past his cock. "I wonder..."

His dark brows came together for a moment before his eyes flew open. "Nick! No! Don't you—"

Biting my lower lip, I slipped the ice cube between his cheeks and ran it around his rim.

"Oh my fucking god!" He dug his heels into the mattress and tried to scoot away from me but I grabbed his thighs and dragged him back into my lap.

"Have you learned your lesson yet?"

"What lesson?" he asked, practically panting.

"You're mine. And from now on, you're not going to do anything to hurt yourself."

"Yes," he said quickly. "Lesson learned. Now, will you please untie me?"

I nodded and the ribbon fell away from his wrists.

He threw himself forward so fast, that I hardly even saw him coming. Slamming me into the mattress, he pinned my wrists above my head, mimicking the pose I'd kept him in. "Since we're being honest, here's a little something for you. If you leave me again, I'll show you what a psycho stalker really looks like. I don't care if I have to fly to the North Pole or wherever the fuck you actually live. I will hunt you down and drag you back here and tie *your* ass up until spring."

"Good. We're in agreement, then." I shifted my hips against him, our cocks rubbing against one another in an obscene version of a handshake.

"You got any other demands?"

"Yeah."

"What?"

"Kiss me."

A wolfish smile crossed his lips. He crushed his mouth against mine, but this time *he* was the one who tasted like peppermint. I licked the remnants of the candy off his mouth before dipping my tongue inside for the rest. His hands slid into my hair, holding me at an angle so he could suck on my tongue.

I moaned against his lips, my fingers digging into his back to pull him as close as I possibly could.

He released my tongue with a sigh and pressed another kiss to my lips briefly, moving on to the side of my neck. There was nothing rushed in his movements. Each kiss was languid, matching the slow glide of his hand over my body.

Planting a trail of kisses from my neck, across my shoulder and chest, he slowly worked his way down until he got to my cock, already flushed and rigid. Lapping at just the head, he licked and swirled and sucked until I was actually writhing, trying to get him to go deeper.

Wrapping his lips around my shaft, he chuckled, sending a wave of vibrations through me. I ran my hand through his dark hair, groaning and thrusting upward in pure desperation.

"I need you," I whispered, fully aware of how the tables had turned and how pathetic I sounded.

"You're so impatient," he said, tsking me as he slid up my body again and kissed me.

"I can't help it."

Slanting his mouth over mine, he grabbed a pillow and dragged it closer. I arched up for him so he could shove it under my hips. With his lips still locked to mine and my hands tangled in his hair, he maneuvered his cock against me. I kissed him harder as he pressed inside, igniting that delicious burn I'd been deprived of for so long.

My breathing came in short bursts the deeper he went until he was completely flush with me.

He groaned into our kiss as he sank down so we were chest-to-chest. We stayed like that for I don't know how long, kissing and savoring the feeling of being connected so completely once again. The way it *should* have been all along.

Even after he started thrusting, we couldn't stop kissing. Everything was slow and sensual, like we both had all the time in the world. Instead of chasing our release in a desperate, frenzied fashion, we sauntered after it, getting distracted along the way by kissing and caressing each other.

The pressure built steadily, like a spring coiling tighter. Caspar must have felt it too because he started thrusting a little quicker, a little harder and both our breath was a little more labored.

He pushed himself upward a bit, giving me the room to reach between us and stroke myself.

"I'm almost there," he panted, his forehead pressed to mine.

"Me too."

Capturing my mouth again, he kissed me hard, driving into me with each snap of his hips.

The spring inside of me shattered, releasing all the tension that had been steadily mounting. I cried out against his lips, shooting proof of my climax between us.

Caspar gave two more thrusts before he pulled out. Biting his lip, he jerked himself quickly, adding his release to the mess on my abdomen with a series of grunts and gasps.

Breathing hard, he slid the pillow out from beneath me and tossed it to the side. He tugged the top sheet up and wiped my skin off before kicking it off the bed and laying down, pressing his cheek to my chest.

"Shower?" I asked, playing idly with his hair and hoping his answer would be "No." As much as I loved our first time in the shower, I didn't know if I had the strength to stand.

He nodded. "Yeah. I just need a minute."

"Take all the time you need."

"You know what's crazy?" Caspar said after a minute, tracing random patterns on my chest.

"What?"

"I love you too."

Caspar

CHAPTER NINE

"You broke my snow globe," I said with a frown. It came out of the blue while we were laying there, tangled together after our shower beneath a clean flannel sheet, since we were both still too hot for the heavy comforter. It's not like I killed the mood since the mood was currently in rest mode, but I'm sure I should have just kept my damn mouth shut.

"I'll get you another one." Nick pressed a soft kiss to my lips, like an apology. "And please don't filter yourself. I always want you to be honest with me. About everything."

"Ok, so *why* did you do it? Were you *that* pissed?"

"No... I'm sorry it seemed that way." If it was possible, he managed to wrap his arm around me even tighter, brushing a kiss to my temple. "The last time I was here and I left, suddenly, it was because my father summoned me back. I had to break it to make sure he couldn't find me again. Or, find me as easily, at any rate."

"What does the snow globe have to do with it?"

"Do you remember seeing me on the railroad tracks?"

Everything was honestly a little fuzzy, but I nodded. "Yeah. I figured I was hallucinating."

"You weren't. That was *me*. You were seeing *me*, talking to me, through the globe. I know... It sounds crazy, but that snow globe and all of the ones made in Winterwald have magic. So, he was able to use it to track me down and he then pulled me away while you were at the door."

My brows dipped. "Pulled you away? He was *here*?"

"No, he used his magic. The same way I can appear and move you around? He can do the same thing."

"Who *are* you people?" I blinked at him. I'd pretty much accepted life as I knew it would never be the same since Nick came around the second time, what with the mind-reading and teleporting or whatever it was, but he never did offer a full explanation.

A half-smile curved his lips and he glanced away. "You're such a skeptic, I know you're not going to believe me."

"Try me." I smirked and nudged him with my elbow.

"We are descended from Saint Nicholas."

I raised my brows at him. "Is that supposed to mean something?"

"Well... that means my father is... um, Father Christmas." He winced as the answer rolled off his tongue.

Staring at him for a minute, I waited to see if he was joking. He, in turn, kept watching me, visibly cringing. When he didn't crack a smile or say anything else, I got the feeling he was telling the truth.

"Are you shitting me?" Pushing myself up into a sitting position, I couldn't help but gape at him. "Father Christmas as in fucking Santa Claus?!"

He nodded slowly and sat up with me, pulling the sheet around his waist.

What the fuck was I supposed to say to that?!

I raked a hand through my hair, trying to make sense of

what he said. He was right, I *was* a skeptic. I hated Christmas and all of the bullshit trappings, the expectations, and the disingenuousness.

But Nick was proof of something... otherworldly. The way he came and went without a trace, the vintage clothes, the snow globe. His goddamn peppermint skin! Who tasted like peppermint around the clock? Unless he bathed every hour in mint body wash, it was impossible.

"Nick," I said slowly, lifting my gaze to his. "As in Nicholas, short for *Saint* Nicholas, which is another name for Santa Claus?"

He gave a small nod, his dark blue eyes glimmering. There's no way a normal person's eyes looked like that. It was almost like there was a meteor shower or falling snow being reflected back at me. It was so beautiful and so *not* natural.

"So... what does that mean for you? Your future?" I hated how my stomach flipped and my lungs spasmed painfully while I waited for his answer. Did that mean he was immortal? Did that mean one day he was going to be the head of the whole fucking Christmas shit show? Like a mafia don, except with elves and tinsel?

"No, I'm not immortal. And yes, he wants me to take over," Nick said in answer to my unasked questions. I must have made a face because he quickly added, "But that's not happening! I don't care. I refuse to bend to his will anymore. Not if it costs me you in the end."

Worrying my lower lip, I tried to figure out why I had a sudden lump in the back of my throat. "But... if you don't do it, what about Christmas?"

"My brother Noel can take over. Or it'll fall to some other descendant somewhere. I don't care. It's not really my problem." His brows furrowed again, matching the downturn of his mouth. "Besides, I thought you hated Christmas?"

"I do," I admitted, suddenly feeling like a horse's ass for

dissing his entire family legacy. Repeatedly. "I mean... There's a lot to hate, don't get me wrong. But that doesn't mean I want kids to be punished for it. Life is already shitty enough. If Christmas is the only thing they can believe in, at least for a little bit, they should get the chance."

Nick smiled and slipped his hand into mine, squeezing it gently. "I wouldn't worry too much about Christmas. It's been around for over sixteen hundred years, as my father likes to remind me. I don't think it's going anywhere anytime soon."

"Yeah? What about you?"

"I told you, I'm here to stay."

"What if your dad pulls you back, like last time?"

"Don't worry. Without the globe, he'll have to find me the old-fashioned way and he's way too busy right now to do that." He leaned forward and pressed his lips to mine, silencing the doubt rampaging in my head.

I slid my fingers through his hair and held the back of his head before flopping into the pillow, pulling him down with me.

CHRISTMAS MORNING.

The bane of my existence had finally arrived. The day that served as a reminder of how utterly alone I was in the world. Would it be as fucked up as last year? Would that glimmer of hope and happiness in my chest be snuffed out the second I opened my eyes?

My head was pounding before I even cracked my eyes open in search of the answer to my silent questions. Squinting past the shafts of sunlight streaming in, I inhaled and stretched.

Something warm and solid shifted against me.

I jerked back, eyes wide, trying to process what I was seeing.

It was Nick.

Nick was still there. Nick actually stayed the whole night. Holy shit!

For his part, Nick blinked and rubbed one eye, his brow furrowing. "Are you ok?"

Watching him warily, I leaned forward and poked him in the chest.

Nick's eyebrows shot up. "What are you doing?"

"Seeing if you're real or if I'm still drunk."

He smirked and surged forward, tackling me into the pillows. Kissing me soundly, he pulled back when we were both out of breath. "Convinced yet?"

"I'm not sure. Could you try that again?"

Grinning, he kissed me again and again; my lips, my chin, my cheeks, all over my face before landing a final kiss on my nose.

"Is this supposed to be a Christmas miracle or something?" I asked, threading my fingers through his hair and pushing it off his forehead.

"No. This is life. *Our* life. Starting now."

I shook my head, even though I felt my lips curving up into a smile. "This is crazy."

"Probably."

"So now what?"

He frowned, genuinely looking perplexed. "I don't know. For us, Christmas morning wasn't exactly a special day. Father sleeps, so the rest of my family goes about their business like normal. We have a big dinner. But that's it."

"So the royal family of Christmas family doesn't *celebrate* Christmas?"

Nick shook his head. "Nope."

"Wow. That's... interesting." And kinda depressing. Your father is the epitome of Christmas and yet you don't get any of the perks? Fuck that!

"How about we start simple and make breakfast? Then we can go from there?"

"Yeah, that sounds good." I smiled and kissed him before rolling out of bed. I tugged on a t-shirt and jeans, hurrying over to the fireplace. Tossing the last of the logs inside the hearth, I dusted my hands off and snagged one of my flannels from the back of a kitchen chair. "I'm going to grab some more."

"I'll start the coffee," Nick said, appearing fully dressed in a dark green sweater and jeans.

I screeched to a halt, doing a double-take. It was the first time I'd seen him in "normal" clothes instead of what he usually wore.

"What?" Nick asked, looking down at himself and running a hand over the cable-knit. "Does it look bad?"

"No. You look great."

He smiled and carried on into the kitchen, moving around the space without any assistance from me. Watching him, already so at ease, it was like he was meant to be here. Maybe I should pinch myself to make sure I wasn't having a super-long, super-detailed dream. Then again, if it was a dream, I sure as hell didn't want to wake up from it.

Forcing myself out the door, I circled around the side of the cabin with the canvas log carrier in hand. I didn't even know if two people *could* comfortably live here. Guess we'd find out. I could always knock out a wall in the spring and add on to the back if he wanted to.

Stacking wood inside the carrier, I glanced inside and

stopped again, watching Nick through the window above the kitchen sink.

For the first time in my life, I looked through the frost-covered glass and smiled like an idiot. Because for the first time in my life it wasn't my grim reflection staring back at me in the windowpane. There was someone else on the other side, who looked up and smiled so brightly it made my heart stutter. I wasn't about to run through the streets like Scrooge after his epiphany, but I cherished the foreign feeling anyway.

A faint jingling of bells sounded through the barren woods while I stacked the last of the logs. Jesus. My daydreaming must have kicked into overdrive when I wasn't paying attention. I couldn't let myself get carried away just because Nick was still there. This could all very well be another dream, as I'd previously thought, or it could be the last few seconds before the train crushed my skull.

Except, if it *was* a dream, why would Nick be screaming?

And why the fuck was he looking at me like that? His eyes were so wide that he looked absolutely horrified.

In a split second, Nick materialized outside with me. No coat, no shoes. Just him.

He reached for my hand, that panicked look frozen on his face as something snagged my shirt from behind.

I stretched my fingers toward Nick, but no matter how hard I tried to reach him, he kept slipping further away until he disappeared completely.

The next thing I knew, I plunged face-first into the Dead River. Aptly named, since that's where I'd planned to kill myself for years and now it appeared I was going to get my wish.

Except, I didn't want to die anymore. I don't even think I wanted to die before. I just didn't want to be alone, so removing myself from the equation seemed like it was the easiest option.

Sensing its imminent demise, the freezing cold shocked my animal brain into action.

Thrashing under the weight, I managed to knock away whatever the fuck was pushing my head under the water. As soon as I felt the pressure lift, I scrambled backward on the snowy riverbank. I sucked in gulps of frigid air, coughing and sputtering ice water out of my lungs while trying to figure out what the fuck just happened.

An old man with a long, scraggly brown beard stepped in front of me. He jabbed the blunt end of a gnarled staff into the center of my chest. Like I was a giant bug, he quite literally tried to skewer me to the ground with the thing, the tiny bells on his long brown coat jingling with the movement.

"Who the fuck are you?!" I asked, grabbing the staff with both hands before he could impale me. Gritting my teeth, I tried to push it off or at least alleviate the stabbing pain radiating through my chest. If *this* was Santa, Christmas was more fucked up than I thought.

Instead of answering, the guy plucked the staff out of my hands and swung it over his head. He brought it down hard and fast, right at my face.

Before it could make contact, something warm and solid landed on top of me.

The world blurred and a multitude of colors swirled around me.

I flopped into another pile of snow, nowhere near the river or the guy who clearly had a grudge against me.

"Are you ok?" Nick asked from on top of me, his eyes wide with worry. "Did he hurt you?"

"I'm fine. Who the fuck was that? Was that your dad?"

He helped me to my feet, dusting snow off my back. "No. That was Rupert."

"Rupert?" I blinked at him. I didn't recall any 'Ruperts' from any Christmas story I'd ever heard of. "Who the fuck is

Rupert? And why the hell did he try to drown me in the river?"

"That's what he does. Be thankful he didn't try to eat you."

"Eat me?!"

"It's a long story. Short version? My dad must have figured out I'm gone and he sent Rupert to kill you and take your soul to Hell."

I opened my mouth to ask a fuck-ton more questions, but a faraway jingling made us both freeze in place.

"We have to go." Nick grabbed my arm and did his weird magic-trip thingie, dumping us in another part of the forest.

My head swam and my stomach felt like it was on a tilt-a-whirl. "I'm gonna puke."

"I'm sorry." He rubbed my back in small, soothing circles while searching the snow-covered landscape, like a rabbit on the lookout for a fox. With his brown coat, that Rupert guy had the perfect camouflage against the dark trees. He could have been anywhere and we'd probably never see him. "I have to get you somewhere safe. Just for a little bit, until I can deal with him."

"Safe from a cannibal hitman sent by Santa Claus? Does that place even exist?"

"Not here. We have to—"

Nick pitched forward with a yelp a second before I was knocked backward in the opposite direction.

Rupert stood between us. Unlike last time, he didn't try to stab me first. A furious snarl twisted his face as he raised the staff, cracking it against the side of my head with way more force than an old man should have.

A shock of pain ricocheted through my brain. The snow next to me was painted red, renewing the surge of bile up the back of my throat. My vision blurred as I picked up my head, but I had to move. I had to get the fuck out of there. But first I had to find Nick.

I could only make out the color of Nick's sweater as he lunged across the distance, slamming into Rupert. They both toppled to the ground, rolling in the snow and grappling for possession of the staff.

Nick was younger, but Rupert was bigger. It didn't take long for Rupert to gain the upper hand. Heaving his weight down on top of Nick, the staff inched closer and closer to Nick's throat. Ice snapped and crackled, spreading along the wood and up Rupert's arms.

I forced myself to roll over and got to my hands and knees in time to see Nick flip Rupert off of him. They were on their feet in a flash, Rupert charging at me and Nick sprinting after Rupert.

Rupert raised the staff again, his black eyes flashing.

All I could do was throw my arm up to shield my face. If I was lucky, all I'd get was a broken forearm. If not, well, I hoped I at least gave the asshole food poisoning if he did end up eating me.

Nick shouted as a wall of ice sprang up in front of me.

Rupert's staff slammed into the opposite side, cracking the ice but not knocking it down.

Exhaling a shaky breath, I stood on wobbly legs and stumbled back a few steps. On the other side of the wall, the brown and green blobs attacked each other again. From this vantage, I couldn't even tell who was winning.

Before I could figure it out, a loud *snap* echoed through the woods. Like the crack of a whip or a bone splitting. Whatever it was, it was loud and *not* fucking good.

A spray of red shot across the ice wall and someone howled in pain, ending with a sputtering gurgle.

"Nick!" My gaze darted from right to left, trying to figure out which was the shortest route to him. I took off as fast as I could for the far end of the wall, stumbling through the snow. My head thumped painfully and my lungs burned from the cold and whatever water was still in there.

As I rounded the corner, I slammed head-first into something.

Collapsing in the snow again, I almost cried when I smelled peppermint. And it was a pair of green arms that wrapped around me, not brown.

"Nick!" I squeezed him tightly, able to finally take a full breath despite the burning. "Are you ok? What happened?" There were speckles of blood on his face, which made him look oddly festive. As much as I dreaded it, I picked my head up and looked in the direction of the blood.

Rupert was laying in a heap, unmoving. From the arc of blood on the ice and the way red was leeching into the snow like a macabre snow cone, it was safe to say the threat was eliminated. The staff had been snapped in two. One half laid on the ground. The jagged point of the other was shoved up underneath Rupert's jaw. Part of it was actually sticking out from the inside of his mouth.

Christ! I thought a little kink was as far as Nick's dark side went. I didn't realize underneath that boyish smile and sparkling, anime eyes he was a fucking savage.

Nick chuckled softly. "I told you. If anyone's going to hurt you, it's going to be *me* — not my uncle."

"That was your uncle?!" How many more bombshells was he going to drop on me in a twenty-four-hour period?

"Yeah. He's not as popular as Father is, for obvious reasons, but there's always been a dark side to Santa Claus. Over time, people just chose to forget."

"And I thought *I* had a fucked-up family life."

"You ready to go home?"

"Most definitely." I got to my feet and held my hands out to him, helping pull him up. Once we were vertical, I dragged the edge of my sleeve across his lips, wiping away the flecks of blood. "There."

He smiled and glanced away, a faint pinkness in his cheeks. "Thanks." Someone shouldn't look so fucking cute after murdering another person, but he did.

As soon as Nick glanced my way, I pressed my lips to his. No one had ever fought for me before in *any* regard, let alone to this extent. Maybe we both had a screw loose, but I didn't care. He was right. We were two sides of the same coin. The same dented, scratched, corroded-as-fuck coin. And it made me so stupidly happy.

Nick

CHAPTER TEN

The happiness with Caspar didn't last.

He'd no more than had the thought, finally realizing what I'd known for what felt like a lifetime, when the horrible prickling crawled across my skin.

"Oh, no..." I shoved Caspar away from me as hard as I could, but he clung to my forearm, his fingers twisted in the sleeve of my sweater.

"What's wrong?"

"Run! Get as far away from me as possible! I'll find you!"

"I'm not leaving you!" Caspar's arms latched around me, which was the complete *opposite* of what he was *supposed* to be doing. Why couldn't he ever listen?!

And now it was too late.

The colors in the bleak landscape blurred and exploded into a million shards, like glass shattering.

I hugged Caspar as hard as I could, burying my face in the side of his neck.

When the swirl of luminescence around us settled, we found ourselves in the frozen courtyard of my father's castle

— a towering structure of cold gray stone and ice, just like him.

Father stood on the steps, glaring down at us with unmasked rage, while the rest of Winterwald looked on from the safety of their doorways and windows. Despite the audience, I knew I was on my own. No one would stand with me if it meant standing against Father.

Turning to face my father, I squared my shoulders and made sure Caspar was fully behind me. He didn't let go of me though, clenching my hand in his so tightly it started to hurt.

"What the..." Caspar whispered, his breath warm on the back of my neck. "Holy shit..."

"This is an outrage!" Father roared, so loud it shook an icicle free from the edge of a roofline. The frozen water plummeted to the ground, shattering on impact. "You brought a mortal here?!"

"*You* brought him here!" I shouted back. "You summoned *me* and I was with Caspar. It's not my fault your magic transported him as well."

"Where is Ruprecht? He was supposed to deal with this."

"Dead." I took immense pleasure in watching Father's eyes widen and then narrow. "And I'll kill the next one, and the one after that. Do you hear me?! I will slay every single one of your dark companions until you get it through your fucking head that I've made my choice and I choose Caspar! You've kept us apart long enough!"

"Then you have condemned the both of you!" Father reached inside his long, fur-trimmed robe and withdrew a silver handbell, eliciting a series of gasps and outcries from the onlookers.

My spine stiffened and my heart pounded wildly in my chest. Tightening my grip on Caspar's hand, I refused to look away or yield in any fashion. I'd already come this far. There was no way I would give him up now, no matter the cost.

Father once said you had to make sacrifices for the greater good and I'd sacrifice everything for Caspar, without question.

"The bell that was rung at the hour of your birth can always be *un*rung, Nicholas. Is that what you want?"

"I want Caspar."

"So be it."

I couldn't help the trembling that spread from my chest outward as Father lifted his hand even higher, making a grand show of my undoing. More than one person slammed their door or shuttered their windows. Would he really follow through? And would I be able to live with the consequences of my decision?

"What's he doing?" Caspar whispered. "What's going on?"

I didn't have time to answer him.

With one flick of his wrist, Father *un*rung the bell as he threatened. Instead of the delicate silver chiming, an ominous clang sounded when the clapper struck the casting, shaking the very ground on which we stood.

The tingling sensation I was used to spread over my skin, growing more pronounced until it felt like claws were ripping into me, flaying my skin open from the inside out. Silver wisps and glittering blue particles tore out of my body, rushing back to the bell they'd originally come from.

I dropped to my knees and doubled over in agony. Gritting my teeth as long as I could, I stifled the scream I knew Father would be pleased to hear, until it, too, tore out of me, echoing off the stone walls.

Caspar knelt and reached for me, but the magic pouring out of me knocked him backward. He called my name, barely audible over my own screaming.

"Klaus! What have you done?!" My mother's voice rang out over the courtyard.

If Father answered, I didn't hear it. As soon as the last

speck of magic slipped away, I pitched face-first onto the frozen cobblestones. Unable to move, I panted through the aftershocks of the pain, trying to remember how to breathe.

Caspar was there in a heartbeat, rolling me over. He cradled my head in his lap, looking me up and down with tears in his eyes. "Nick! Are you ok? What did he do to you?"

I couldn't even answer. My throat was raw from all the screaming. Instead, I reached for his hand. As soon as Caspar saw what I wanted, he slipped his hand into mine and held it tightly. I clung to it like a life preserver, buoyed by his presence alone.

"He has forsaken us!" Father thundered.

"So you disown him?" My mother shouted in return. "You take back his magic? You look over children around the world and yet you treat your son with such callousness! What kind of a father are you?"

"One who will not tolerate anyone tarnishing this family!"

"The way you've tarnished it?" a third voice called out.

Noel.

I craned my head, looking for him as the crowd began to slowly reappear. My brother appeared in the doorway of the glassblower's shop, his face contorted with outrage.

"Noel, stay out of this," Father snapped.

"No."

"Noel!"

Instead of complying, Noel hoisted a thick, black book in the air, drawing hushed murmurs from the spectators. "You've gone too far, Father. First Rupert? Now Nick? You've lost your way and it's time things changed before *you* destroy the legacy you're so keen to preserve."

Father took a step down the stairs, closer to Noel, like he could stop him from across the courtyard. "Put that down. You don't know what you're doing."

"Burning the Devil's Book so you can't use it as a weapon

anymore? Yes, I do know what I'm doing." Noel pivoted and tossed the heavy tome into the furnace. The ancient leather hissed and squealed as the flames consumed it. A noxious black smoke poured out of the top of the chimney, reeking of brimstone.

All the while, Father stood speechless, staring with horror as the last vestiges of his draconian law were reduced to nothing more than ash. I closed my eyes and let out a grateful sigh. Caspar would be safe. No matter what happened to me now, Caspar and his soul were free.

Noel walked over to us and held a hand out to me. I stared up at my little brother with a newfound wonder before accepting his hand. He and Caspar got me to my feet before Noel turned to face our parents, standing shoulder-to-shoulder with me. Caspar wrapped an arm around my waist, touching his forehead to mine gently.

"Klaus, it's time," Mother said stiffly and held her hand out.

I expected Father to fight. To yell, to bluster, to strip the lot of them of their magic.

Wordlessly, Father gave her the silver bell, his large shoulders rounded in defeat.

Mother snatched it out of his hand and stormed past him. Hurrying down the stairs, her crimson velvet gown swept away the snow where she walked. She stopped in front of us with a grim smile, clutching the bell to her chest. "Nicholas."

"Mother," I replied, swallowing thickly. She'd always understood my plight but until this moment, she'd been unable to do anything. I'm glad she found the courage to finally stand up to him, for her sake, but it was too late to erase the damage she'd already inflicted on our relationship.

"You can stay in Winterwald," she said, her blue eyes glancing at Caspar. "But you know your magic is gone forever. And if you leave here, there's no coming back."

"My life was never here, Mother. Magic or no magic."

She nodded and turned to Noel. "Did you really have to burn the Devil's Book?"

"Yes," Noel said, without even hesitating. "No child should be handed over to the Devil. It was a terrible threat in the Middle Ages and it's still a terrible threat. But at least now that's *all* it is — an empty scare tactic instead of eternal damnation."

She smiled and touched his cheek. "That's my boy." Having passed his test, Mother handed Noel the silver bell with a small nod.

Noel inclined his head in return, handling the bell as gently as possible. There wasn't a shred of doubt my brother was destined to be a better Father Christmas than I ever would have. Maybe under him, Christmas could get back to how it used to be before it had been corrupted by modernity.

"Caspar Payne," Mother said, taking a step to the side so she could stand in front of him directly. "You poor boy. I know you've suffered as well. But I also know my son loves you with his whole heart. Take care of each other and neither of you will ever feel alone again."

"I don't think you have to worry about us," Caspar replied, tightening his arm around my waist.

She wiped a tear from her cheek and sniffed, forcing a smile on her face. "Well, then. You should get going. Noel can send you on your way."

"Goodbye, Mother," I said weakly. I knew it was coming and yet my throat felt like it was seconds away from closing entirely.

She took a step closer and kissed my forehead. "Goodbye, my sweet boy."

I clutched the back of Caspar's shirt, trying not to lose it as my mother walked away. This was what I wanted. Caspar was what I wanted. But I knew from this moment on, I'd never see my family again. Not that I wanted to see my father. Ever. But my mother? My brother? They were collateral damage in my war with *him*. Now they would suffer because one person had ruled this family like a tyrant. No one had been able to stop him until now but now it was too late for a different outcome. Even if I stayed, I'd always feel resentment that things *could have* been different, if only they'd stood up to Father sooner.

Swallowing down a torrent of emotions, I turned to Noel and focused on the most basic feeling I had — gratitude. "Thank you. For what you did."

"You deserve to be happy. So do you," Noel said, peering past me to Caspar. "Go and live your best lives."

"Let's go home," Caspar whispered, brushing my tears away with his thumb.

Nodding, I faced him and twined my arms around his neck. I exhaled a slow breath, keeping my gaze focused on Caspar's face. "We're ready."

"Merry Christmas," Noel said as the shimmering silver and blue sparkles enveloped us like a miniature snowstorm, sending us on our way.

Caspar

ONE YEAR LATER

"Here we go again," I muttered, watching a frazzled woman pick up and put down half a dozen items before finally settling on something.

I'd always hated last-minute shoppers during the holidays and this year was no exception. I would try to go about my own business and grab the shit I *actually* needed and inevitably get elbowed out of the way by other people in the mad dash to fill their cart with seasonal delicacies and last-minute presents. But now as a business owner? I really fucking hated them. It's not *my* fault *they* waited to go shopping. Failure to plan accordingly on their part did *not* constitute an emergency on mine. And the whole concept of "the customer is always right" was absolute bullshit. Nine times out of ten the customer was an entitled jackass who could get bent. I was there to sell them a product, not be treated like a second-class citizen.

"Shh." Nick elbowed me gently before turning on his dazzling smile. The woman hurried up to the register with a hand-carved nutcracker. "Is this all for you today?"

"I don't suppose you could make another one? With a red

coat instead of blue? She prefers red," the woman said, glancing between Nick and I, holding up the last nutcracker in the store like we had no idea what she was talking about.

"On December 23rd?" I replied flatly.

"Who are you shopping for? Maybe we can suggest something else?" Nick said over the top of me. This was why he handled the customer-service aspect of the business and I kept my ass in the back of the shop where it was just me and a room full of lumber waiting to be turned into something. I still did the odd construction job here and there, but these days I was usually too busy building furniture and toys and whatever other design Nick threw my way. I might have had the talent for woodworking, but he was the true artist and he was the reason this store existed in the first place.

"My daughter was supposed to spend the holidays with her boyfriend and his family," the woman said, as if anyone actually cared. I mean, I know Nick asked but we didn't need the whole goddamn story. Literally a gender, an age, and how they were connected to you was all he was looking for. "But they broke up so now she's coming home and I hadn't gotten her anything because we weren't planning on seeing her until after the new year."

"Hate those last-minute guests," I said, shaking my head with zero sympathy in my voice.

Nick flew around the counter so fast that I thought his ass was on fire. He gestured to the opposite end of the store. "There's a whole assortment of music boxes over here. I don't know if you saw them."

"Oh, no. I didn't." The woman toddled off in the direction Nick was guiding her. As soon as she turned her back, he threw a glance over his shoulder, giving me one of his exasperated looks.

I shrugged and retreated to my workshop to pack up my tools. This was our last working day and then the store would be closed until the new year. Was it "bad" for a fledgling business? Maybe. Did we give a shit? Absolutely not. We had every intention of holing up at home and avoiding everyone for a week of much-deserved rest, since holidays were meant to be enjoyed and all that.

One thing we'd agreed on when it came to *any* holiday was that we were only doing the parts of it that resonated with us. If it meant we skipped an entire holiday, then we skipped an entire holiday. Who cared? It worked for us.

So far Valentine's Day was a hard pass, except for the chocolate-covered strawberries Nick brought home from the confectionary down the street. I was more than ok with those. St. Patrick's had been a hit (because, alcohol). Easter was a total pass. Memorial Day and Fourth of July were both in the "Yes" column thanks to the grilling out (and the alcohol). Halloween was a massive hit, as was Thanksgiving. And Christmas? Christmas had yet to be determined.

We both agreed to skip the store-bought decorations. I was fine not decorating at all, but Nick wanted to do *something*, so we spent an afternoon walking through the woods and collecting branches for him to make garland out of. And by "him," he really meant both of us because stringing live garland around the cabin was a two-person job.

I helped him shove cloves in oranges and even let him use my smoker to dry out even *more* oranges and cranberries. I drew the line at real candles in the windows, though, despite his lengthy monologue about the history of candles and Christmas trees. I didn't have visions of Tannenbaum in my head — only our fucking house going up in flames. So, the little pyro agreed to light them at night when we were home and I had a fire extinguisher on standby.

We also said no to exchanging presents. Even with the addition we built in the beginning half of the year, the cabin wasn't *that* big. There was literally no reason to get each other anything when we already had everything we could feasibly want.

After Nick locked up the front of the store, we headed out back and climbed into my truck. As soon as the vehicle was in motion, I reached for his hand. Even with his attention turned out the snowy window, Nick instinctively took my hand in his and laced our fingers together.

We drove home in silence. Not the awkward, pissed-off kind of silence — the companionable kind, the kind two people shared when they were utterly comfortable in one another's presence and didn't feel obligated to fill the quiet with nonsense.

Except, the silence pretty much continued through dinner, all the way until we slid into bed. I had a feeling I knew what it was, but I didn't want to ask. It was right about then that I kind of missed Nick's whole mind-reading thing. It would have saved a lot of effort on my part, trying to figure out how to ask a question without coming off like an asshole.

"You seem sad," I said, figuring I'd aim for a softer opening than blurting out a question.

Nick rolled onto his side and propped his head on his hand. "Just thinking."

"About your family?" Well, so much for not blurting shit out.

He nodded. "I know I'm better off. Please don't think I'm not happy here. I *am* happy. But it's been harder than I thought, seeing all the Christmas stuff and knowing I'm not a part of it anymore."

"Were you really a part of it before, though? I mean... your dad was kind of an asshole."

"He was a major asshole. I remember, as a kid, looking in on happy families getting together and, you know, *genuinely* enjoying each other's company. I always wondered why we didn't do that and why I always got this knot in my chest when December came around. As I got older, you could feel the tension in our house just growing into this monstrous beast the closer we got to Christmas. And then? It's like someone let the steam out of the kettle. I could breathe until it started all over again. But I don't feel that this year, that knot."

I ran my palm over his chest, rubbing it in small circles. "You'll tell me if you do, right?"

"Of course. We tell each other everything."

"I know... I just don't want you to resent me because *I'm* the reason you're not with your family anymore."

He leaned closer, touching his forehead to mine and cupping my cheek. "Caspar, you *are* my family. Leaving was my choice. Just because I'm a little nostalgic for how things used to be doesn't mean I regret choosing you. I'm missing the familiarity of what *was*, but that in no way diminishes my love for you or the excitement I feel for what's to come."

Just like the Grinch, my heart tripled in size. I intended to brush my lips across his in a gentle kiss, but the moment our mouths touched I pounced on him. Licking the seam of his lips, I dipped my tongue in as soon as they parted, meeting his halfway to swirl with mine.

He carded his fingers through my hair with both hands, holding onto the sides of my head so he could pull back and look at me. "Before you get carried away, I have something for you."

"I hope it's that hot drink/ice cube thing you do. It's kind of grown on me."

He might have rolled his eyes, but he still grinned. "No, but I'll keep that in mind. Check under your side of the bed."

I gave his angelic face the side-eye for a minute before shifting off of him and leaning over the side of the bed. Groping beneath the frame, I finally found a box. I tried to pick it up with one hand, but it was heavier than shit, so I needed both to haul it up or risk dropping it.

It was a Christmas present. I mean, I kind of had a feeling when he said to look under the bed and then had that innocent smile. But I didn't expect a beautifully wrapped red and gold package with a ridiculously fancy bow.

"We said no—"

"It's not what you think," Nick butted in.

"If it looks like a Christmas present and it feels like a Christmas present..."

"Then it must be an *anniversary* present." He waggled his brows and bit his lower lip. The angel was gone, replaced with a self-satisfied devil. "Just open it."

Huffing, I slid the ornate ribbon off and tore into the paper, revealing a plain cardboard box with zero indication as to what was inside. Lifting the lid, I dug through the packing peanuts until my fingers touched cold glass.

My gaze snapped to his, widening slightly. "You didn't."

"I did."

Pulling my hand out of the box, I unearthed the snow globe within, smiling like an idiot.

It wasn't as fancy as the one he'd given me before, but I felt pretty safe in the knowledge no one was using it as a means to magically spy on us. Besides, as nice as the ice castle was to look at, I liked the inside of this one a thousand times better.

Sitting atop a carved wooden base, the little scene inside the new snow globe was an exact replica of our cabin, surrounded by pine trees. I tipped it over and righted it again, watching the swirl of white and silver snowflakes. It was absolutely perfect. I'd never been so happy to receive a gift in my life, even if Nick was splitting hairs on the whole anniversary versus Christmas thing.

The clock on the mantel chimed twelve, breaking through my happy little bubble. I was actually grateful for the distraction. It saved me from doing something totally uncool, like cry. Over a present.

"Happy anniversary," Nick said softly, caressing the side of my face.

"Happy anniversary," I whispered back. Pressing my lips to his, I reached past him and set the snow globe on the nightstand. Once my hands were free, I tangled them in his hair and kissed him in earnest.

Once upon a time, I'd questioned if Nick coming into my life was some sort of Christmas miracle.

His answer still made me smile.

No. This is life. Our life.

And we were going to make the most of it. Together.

Epilogue

And so, Nick and Caspar got their happily ever after. Yet unlike the fairytales would have you believe, it was because they worked for it every single day. It wasn't a grand life, filled with riches and luxury. But it was *their* life — one they built together and one they wouldn't trade for anything.

As time went on, they formed their own traditions, their own rituals. They took the best of the holidays and made them their own. People may have questioned their refusal to participate in the commercial trappings of Christmas but at the end of the day it was no one else's life and thus none of their concern, as Nick liked to politely remind them. Caspar, on the other hand, told the opinionated denizens of Coventry in no uncertain terms to "Fuck off."

In a society driven by the need to produce and perform around the clock, it was hard to understand how one could be happy collecting pine boughs every year instead of stringing artificial lights and setting up inflatable snowmen. It was hard to understand why a specially-prepared meal meant more than a store-bought gift that would sit on a shelf, unused, until it

"My life was never here, Mother. Magic or no magic."

She nodded and turned to Noel. "Did you really have to burn the Devil's Book?"

"Yes," Noel said, without even hesitating. "No child should be handed over to the Devil. It was a terrible threat in the Middle Ages and it's still a terrible threat. But at least now that's *all* it is — an empty scare tactic instead of eternal damnation."

She smiled and touched his cheek. "That's my boy." Having passed his test, Mother handed Noel the silver bell with a small nod.

Noel inclined his head in return, handling the bell as gently as possible. There wasn't a shred of doubt my brother was destined to be a better Father Christmas than I ever would have. Maybe under him, Christmas could get back to how it used to be before it had been corrupted by modernity.

"Caspar Payne," Mother said, taking a step to the side so she could stand in front of him directly. "You poor boy. I know you've suffered as well. But I also know my son loves you with his whole heart. Take care of each other and neither of you will ever feel alone again."

"I don't think you have to worry about us," Caspar replied, tightening his arm around my waist.

She wiped a tear from her cheek and sniffed, forcing a smile on her face. "Well, then. You should get going. Noel can send you on your way."

"Goodbye, Mother," I said weakly. I knew it was coming and yet my throat felt like it was seconds away from closing entirely.

She took a step closer and kissed my forehead. "Goodbye, my sweet boy."

I clutched the back of Caspar's shirt, trying not to lose it as my mother walked away. This was what I wanted. Caspar was what I wanted. But I knew from this moment on, I'd never see my family again. Not that I wanted to see my father. Ever. But my mother? My brother? They were collateral damage in my war with *him*. Now they would suffer because one person had ruled this family like a tyrant. No one had been able to stop him until now but now it was too late for a different outcome. Even if I stayed, I'd always feel resentment that things *could have* been different, if only they'd stood up to Father sooner.

Swallowing down a torrent of emotions, I turned to Noel and focused on the most basic feeling I had — gratitude. "Thank you. For what you did."

"You deserve to be happy. So do you," Noel said, peering past me to Caspar. "Go and live your best lives."

"Let's go home," Caspar whispered, brushing my tears away with his thumb.

Nodding, I faced him and twined my arms around his neck. I exhaled a slow breath, keeping my gaze focused on Caspar's face. "We're ready."

"Merry Christmas," Noel said as the shimmering silver and blue sparkles enveloped us like a miniature snowstorm, sending us on our way.

was either thrown out or re-gifted to some other unfortunate soul.

And while many people will wax poetically about the "true meaning of Christmas," Nick and Caspar are here to remind you that the meaning of Christmas — or any holiday, for that matter — is up to *you* to decide. It's your life, your rules.

So, when the Susans of the world get on your case, you can tell them exactly what they can do with their sugar plum danishes and peppermint mocha lattes. They can fuck right off.

Author's Note

I honestly didn't think I'd ever write a Christmas story. Or a novella. But I have to say I had a blast with Nick and Caspar! They filled my little Grinchy heart with so much love this holiday season and I hope they can do the same for you, no matter when you're reading this.

What started as a casual remark by a reader turned into this little pet project and it absolutely blossomed. She, like so many others, wanted to see a different sort of Christmas story. An anti-Christmas story, if you will. One that isn't another fluffy rom-com, involving a healthy dose of cheese and eye-rolling. And if that's your jam, great. You're probably *not* reading this one then. But if you love the fluff and you *are* reading this, that's great too. Because Christmas (and life) *is* what you make it.

Churches will tell you how to live your life.

Corporations will tell you how to live your life.

Susan will tell you how to live your life.

But you're the only one living it, so live it how you want. Just remember, whatever you're feeling during the holidays is completely valid. Whether you love Christmas, hate Christmas, or are somewhere in between, it's *all* valid and you're not as alone as you think. You can cut off toxic family and still miss them. It's ok. You can see happy, healthy families and be sad you don't have the same thing. It's ok. You can be stressed over money and forced gatherings and a thousand other things. It's ok. Christmas takes a lot of fucking work, especially when the world is telling you how you "should" be celebrating. It's ok to feel all the feels and just want to hibernate until the new year. No one gets to tell you how to feel and if they try to? Well, you know what Caspar would say.

P.S. There's so much Christmas symbolism in this bad boy, the nerd in me is geeking the fuck out. I am immensely proud of myself for how I was able to weave everything together. There are Easter eggs galore! Little nods to the season sprinkled throughout. It's like the history of Christmas packed into a tiny little novella. So at the very least, if you don't walk away from this book feeling validated or entertained, hopefully you can take away some trivial bit of Christmas knowledge. My totally useless gift to you. You're welcome.

Acknowledgments

So normally I have no idea what to write in these, but this time I *absolutely* know who to thank!

First and foremost, Lori — for presenting me with this little nugget of an idea. As you can see, I *ran* with it. I hope you love what I came up with.

Amy — at this point, I feel like I should be paying you to be my therapist or at least my crisis counselor. Every time I'm on a ledge, you talk me down from it. You have this quiet, steady strength about you that just calms me down. I don't think I can write any book without getting your opinion. You have no idea how much I value you!

Stefka — your encouragement and support has been much appreciated throughout this whirlwind project! The pictures have been very motivational as well. I love getting messages from you, even if I have to make sure no one is looking when I open them.

Gloria — the love and enthusiasm you have for this little book and these boys is amazing! You're the one who convinced me it actually *should* see the light of day. But I think you're right. There is a market for grimmer versions of Christmas, instead of the Hallmark/Disney variety we've been taught is the standard.

Julia — I know novellas aren't your thing, but I still couldn't have done this one without you. I love your honesty and your critical eye. It goes without saying that it helps to have a level head look at your work and point out areas in need of strengthening. So thank you for making time during this crazy time of year to give your feedback!

About the Author

Award-winning dark romance author Ashlyn Drewek has always been a hopeless romantic. She's also fascinated by the dark, macabre things in life (you can blame a love of Halloween and Edgar Allan Poe for that one).

Most of her time is spent making up stories in her head or researching some obscure topic just because she's that much of a nerd. The degree on the wall says she's a historian, but the paycheck says she's a first responder.

Ashlyn lives in Northern Illinois with her patient husband, fearless daughter, and a house full of animals.

For information on news and upcoming releases, check out her website at www.ashlyndrewek.com to sign up for her newsletter or follow her at any of the social media options below.

Also by Ashlyn Drewek

The Leander Welles Series:

THE MYSTERY OF LEANDER WELLES — a dark, psychological romantic suspense about a criminal psychiatrist who falls in love with her patient. Finalist for Suspense in the 2021 Next Generation Indie Book Awards.

THE RATIONALE OF LEANDER WELLES — a dark, psychological romantic suspense about an alleged murderer who falls in love with his psychiatrist... or does he?

THE DAMNATION OF LEANDER WELLES: OR, THE DEATH & LIFE OF BENNETT REEVE — a dark MM friends-to-lovers romance about a cutthroat lawyer and an enigmatic millionaire and what happens when two dark souls join forces. A prequel to Book I and II.

THE WRATH OF LEANDER WELLES — a dark, MM romantic suspense about love, revenge, and how far a psychopath is willing to go for both.

THE FALL OF LEANDER WELLES — TBD

The Solnyshko Duet:

THE KIDNAPPING OF ROAN SINCLAIR — a dark MM romance about an American college guy who is kidnapped by a Russian criminal.

THE VENGEANCE OF ROAN SINCLAIR — a dark MM romance about love in the aftermath of trauma and finding your new normal.

MM Contemporary Standalone:

THE DELIVERANCE OF MAREK SOMMERS — TBD

Paranormal & Dark Fantasy:

MALUM DISCORDIAE — a dark academia MM enemies-to-lovers paranormal romance about witches, Necromancers, and a blood feud that has lasted centuries.

THE COVENTRY CAROL — a darker MM Christmas novella with hot Santa smut, anti-Christmas feels, and a cannibal hitman.

PER SANGUINEM — a slow-burn paranormal MM romantic suspense standalone about vampires and cops with commitment issues and what happens when you fall in love with your partner.

www.ingramcontent.com/pod-product-compliance
Lightning Source LLC
Chambersburg PA
CBHW030545130626
46552CB00006B/2424